CEREAL KILLER

A MATERNAL INSTINCTS MYSTERY

DIANA ORGAIN

Lemonade
Press

OTHER TITLES BY DIANA ORGAIN

Third Time's a Crime If only love were as simple as murder...

ROUNDUP CREW MYSTERY SERIES

Yappy Hour Things take a *ruff* turn at the Wine & Bark when Maggie Patterson takes charge

Trigger Yappy Salmonella poisoning strikes at the Wine & Bark.

IWITCH MYSTERY SERIES

A Witch Called Wanda Can a witch solve a murder mystery?

I Wanda put a spell on you When Wanda is kidnapped, Maeve might need a little magic.

Brewing up Murder A witch, a murder, a dog...no, wait...a man..no...two men, three witches and a cat?

COOKING UP MURDER MYSTERY SERIES

Murder as Sticky as Jam Mona and Vicki are ready for the grand opening of Jammin' Honey until...their store goes up in smoke...

Murder as Sweet as Honey Will the sweet taste of honey turn bitter with a killer town?

Murder as Savory as Biscuits Can some savory biscuits uncover the truth behind a murder?

Cereal

Killer

A Maternal Instincts Mystery

by
Diana Orgain

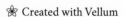 Created with Vellum

CHAPTER 1

"*B*ut what do you *mean* there's no cell service?" I wailed, staring at my phone. Zero bars.

From the driver's seat, Vicente Domingo flashed his trademark smirk. Most women in most situations found his roguish, tall-dark-and-handsome shtick charming. In the best of times, I found it only *mildly* obnoxious.

This was not the best of times.

"No worries," he crooned in his lilting Spanish accent. "I'm sure we won't be stuck on the side of the road too long."

"It's four thousand degrees outside!" I sputtered.

"You're exaggerating by exactly 3900 degrees."

The temperature gauge flicked from 100 to 101. I pointed to it. "Make that three thousand eight hundred and ninety-nine."

"Really—don't worry, *quierda*. I'll pop the hood and see if it's an easy fix." He opened the car door, letting in a *whoosh* of heat.

"I'm not your love," I muttered as he closed the door behind him. I traced the BMW's black leather seat. Shouldn't a car like this be too expensive to break down on us?

When Vicente Domingo—a rival PI—had invited me out to the town of Golden to solve a mystery, I'd been excited . . . and a little confused. But I definitely hadn't planned to end up stranded twenty-seven minutes from our destination, in ten-thousand-degree heat, while more than seven months pregnant with twins!

How busy was this road, exactly?

After passing Sacramento, we took highway 49 toward Golden, but a traffic jam a few miles earlier had sent us onto a back road through the middle of nowhere. I tried to remember how many cars we'd passed in the last few minutes. I hadn't been paying close attention, but I only remembered one other car.

Surely someone would happen upon us soon and we wouldn't roast out here like a pair of Thanksgiving turkeys.

Mmm, Thanksgiving turkey sounds good. My mouth watered at the thought. Darn pregnancy hormones.

A minute later, Vicente popped back in the car, a wave of heat following him.

"Don't let out all the air conditioning," I whined.

He closed the door with a little shrug. "We're about twenty-five minutes from my cousin's house. I'm sure someone will give us a lift. Luz is well known in town, and I've visited enough that someone will recognize me. I spent whole summers here as a boy, when my grandparents owned the winery."

I stared out the window. No trees lined this road, but there was a small grove in the distance. If we ran out of gas and couldn't blast the air conditioning, we'd have to walk to those trees to find shade. I eyed Vicente's biceps.

He'd recovered impressively from a gunshot wound a few months back, but still I doubted he could haul my pregnant rump if my knees gave out.

And also...wasn't this rattlesnake country?

What on earth am I doing here?

A few yards ahead of the car, a huge pile of rocks sat just off the road. I stared at the rock pile, startled. For a second, one of the rocks had looked just like one of those sun-bleached ox skulls they used to set the mood in grim Wild West movies. I blinked a few times, reassuring myself that it was just a white rock and not an omen of impending doom.

"Worst case scenario," Vicente continued, "it's supposed to pour rain sometime this afternoon. That'll cool us off."

I couldn't tell if he was joking or not. Time to focus on something I could control. I rubbed my temples.

The case. Might as well take the opportunity to talk more about the case. "So, why exactly did your cousin want *two* PIs to come investigate this vineyard thing?" I asked.

It was the question that had been nagging at me ever since Vicente had explained the situation—someone was trying to sabotage his cousin's vineyard. First, there had been a few threatening notes. Then an attempted break-in in the middle of the night. Then a ransomware attack on the vineyard's computer system.

The ransomware attack had been the last straw. It hadn't worked—Luz kept careful backups and had replaced her computer rather than pay off the hackers—but she'd called Vicente for help.

After a long pause, he said, "I asked her if I could bring a PI friend with me. Her friends and neighbors know that her cousin is a PI, so people will know something is up if I'm asking too many questions. I figured we could tag-team and keep it quiet that we're investigating anything."

"So we don't tip off the saboteur? Won't they expect Luz to bring someone in to look into it?"

"Well . . . that's *part* of it."

I stared at him for a second. "Why don't we want anyone to know we're investigating?"

He grimaced. "Luz . . . made a mistake with the winery."

Suspicion bloomed in my chest. Crossing my arms, I asked, "What kind of mistake? What have you dragged me into, Vicente?"

He clasped his hands together. "Nothing too terrible. Nothing illegal. This sort of thing really happens all the time, I'm told. Where to start . . ."

"You could always try the beginning," I deadpanned.

"The winery is very profitable. My grandparents bought the vineyard in the 1970s from a winemaker who was struggling to get by, and they turned it into something great. Luz chose to carry on the family business. Turns out she's spectacular at it—she's won several wine-of-the-year awards, that sort of thing. Plus, she's tripled the size of the operation since she took it over. But she lost ninety percent of the harvest this year and opted to buy another vineyard's grapes and make the season's wine anyway—labeled as if it really came from her vineyard."

I sucked in a sharp breath. "Oh . . ."

"It was a rolling blackout. She has a generator, of course, but every vineyard in the region was scrambling for fuel to run the generators, and she couldn't get enough gas in time. So, most of the grapes spoiled."

"How awful," I murmured.

"As I said, the vineyard is profitable, but that much expansion means there is a lot of debt, too. They couldn't afford to lose a whole year. I wish she'd come to me before she made the decision. I would have told her that her name was big enough to ride out the storm—to just raise the prices on the wines that are coming of age, and to bottle what little wine they could eke out of this year's harvest . . . when that's ready to sell, market it as a super-rare special edition for thousands of dollars a bottle. But I guess she . . . was not so confident, or didn't think about that option. Companies order from her years in advance, you see. I can only imagine she was worried about backing out of contracts."

"Mmm," I said softly. "That doesn't make it right, of course, but she was in a hard position."

"Yes, she was." He slumped back against the leather seat. "In one of our conversations about the blackouts, she said to me, 'Vicente, what if it happens again next year?' She decided she needed to add solar panels and batteries to go with them . . . not enough to run the whole vineyard all the time, but enough to keep processing wine in an emergency."

"And that's a huge expense."

"Exactly. So I think she must have been worried about how to pay for it. Would the bank extend her credit if they thought her business was in trouble from a lost harvest? Would they call her existing debts due? I don't know."

"What a mess."

He let out a sigh. "So, that's some background of why we don't want people to know we're investigating. I told you that she received some threatening notes?"

I nodded.

"We'll look at them when we get to her house, but she told me that, whoever this person is, they know she bought someone else's grapes. She thinks that may be the reason they're harassing her."

"A rival vineyard?"

He let out a sigh and turned up the air conditioning. "Maybe. Or maybe an ex-boyfriend. Thomas." His lips curled into a sneer. "I always hated him. Smug idiot. He runs a local wine bar, and he recently expanded his business—bought the building next door to his bar and fixed it up as an all-inclusive wedding venue. Luz's vineyard is beautiful, and people rent it out for events, especially weddings. Thomas is still in love with her and is trying to win her back, but he's also trying to undermine her business and poach her catering and event contracts. It's like he's obsessed with her. The weasel."

"How long ago did they break up?"

"About a year. And good riddance," he muttered.

A white Prius appeared, driving the opposite direction. I clumsily leaped out of the car and waved frantically, but I was too slow; the car passed us by.

With a sigh, I sank back into my seat and closed the door.

"We could always walk," he said.

I pointed to my pregnant belly.

"Then again, maybe not," he conceded.

A horn beeped, and I turned around to see the white Prius pulling in behind us. A heavyset blonde with a chin-length bob climbed out and marched toward Vicente's door.

We're saved!

Sweet relief flooded me.

Vicente rolled down the window. "Hello, *quierda*," he drawled. "Thanks so much for stopping. We stalled out—"

The woman stared at us in unconcealed contempt. "Serves you right driving around that fancy gas-guzzler."

I furrowed my brow, and Vicente glanced at me in utter confusion.

"Gas-guzzler?" he practically sputtered. "This Beamer gets thirty-four miles to the gallon on the highway."

Her eyes bulged. "And do you think that's going to save us from climate change? Did you pay any attention to last year's fire season? To the hurricanes in the South? Why, you—"

"I'm on your side," I interjected, shooting her a winning smile. "Why, this whole trip I've done nothing but try to persuade Vicente to get a more fuel-efficient car. Something like your Prius."

Vicente glared at me, but I ignored him. This woman might be crazy, but so far she was our only ticket out of this mess. If Vicente wouldn't charm some help out of her, I most assuredly would.

I rested a hand on my baby bump. "After all, I'm pregnant with twins! You know what I told this idiot here?" I jerked my elbow toward Vicente. "I said, *What kind of world are we going to leave for our children if we don't all pitch in and do our part?*"

The woman visibly softened.

I continued. "And it's just killing me that we're sitting here and running the engine for the air conditioning—so many useless emissions! But I've had a complicated pregnancy, and my doctor has told me I absolutely can't overheat. Is there any way you might be able to give us a lift into Golden? To Castillo's Vineyard?"

She stared at us for a few seconds, her eyes flashing between annoyance and something kinder. Then she said, "I'm late for a Go-Green meeting in Sacramento, but I'll have cell service in a couple miles, so I'll call a tow truck for you."

Good enough! "Thank you!" I exclaimed. "As soon as we broke down, I sent a plea out into the universe for a good person like you to help us out!"

She tried to hide a grin. "Sure, anytime!" Then she looked at Vicente, and her smile turned to a glower. "And get a car with better gas mileage!"

She stalked back to her Prius, and as soon as Vicente rolled up the window, I burst out laughing.

"What was that?" he demanded.

"*That,*" I retorted, "was creatively getting us a tow truck. You should know. You pull those sorts of tricks all the time—you just do it by flirting and calling everyone *dear* in that accent of yours."

"You threw me under the bus!"

"Under a solar-powered bus, maybe." I grinned. "You're just perplexed that your charm got you absolutely nowhere with her."

"How do you know she'll even call a tow truck? Maybe she'll get madder and madder about my so-called gas-guzzler and change her mind."

"She'll call," I said, hitting the button to recline my seat. "Just you wait."

Sure enough, a half hour later, Vicente swore under his breath. "Well, I'll be."

I sat up. A big white tow truck was rumbling our way.

"Thank goodness!" I sang.

The tow truck parked in front of us, and we both climbed out of the car. Heat waves practically sizzled up from the ground, and I immediately broke out into a sweat.

You could probably fry an egg on this road.

Vicente strode toward the truck, meeting the driver halfway. "Vicente Domingo," he said. "Thanks so much for coming!"

"Fred," replied the driver, reaching out to shake Vicente's hand. He was tall, with sandy-colored hair and a kind demeanor. "Got a call that you folks needed some help."

Vicente looked mournful. "The car broke down. I'm going to my cousin's place—Castillo's Vineyard."

"Oh, you're Luz's cousin," replied Fred, his smile broadening. "It's so nice to meet you!"

"That's right," said Vicente. "And this lovely woman is Kate, my fiancée!"

Fiancée? That's his cover story? I blanched and instinctively reached to touch my wedding ring . . . but I'd taken it off two days ago when the swelling in my hands and ankles had finally reached a breaking point.

Oh, I could kill him.

CHAPTER 2

*I*n the tow truck, Fred turned the key in the ignition. "Why don't I drop you folks off at Luz's place, and then I'll take the car into the mechanic for you. I'll call when I have an update."

"That'd be great," replied Vicente, fiddling with the AC vent. "Really appreciate you coming out so quickly."

"Benefit of being a tow truck driver in a fairly small town—I usually get three or four calls a day from people in the surrounding area, but not so many that I get backed up with multiple urgent calls very often. Which is especially good on a hot day like this. Glad you folks were all right."

I didn't say anything. I was wedged between Fred and Vicente in the cab of the truck, grateful for our ride to the vineyard but still steaming over the cover story Vicente had invented.

Hello, 911? I'd like to report a murder. The victim? My dignity.

I shot Vicente a death glare that burned hotter than the California sun, but he ignored me.

If he expects me to giggle and hold his hand and act like we're in love, he's got another think coming.

The tow truck eased out onto the road. "So," Fred said. "When's the wedding?"

Vicente said, "In a few—"

"We're still discussing that," I interjected coolly. "There's been a little trouble in paradise, I'm afraid."

Out of the corner of my eye, I caught a look of amusement on Vicente's face.

Two can play this game. If he was going to dress me up as his fiancée, I was going to set the terms of the "relationship."

"I'm sorry to hear that," said Fred apologetically. There was an awkward pause. "What brings you out to Golden?"

"Visiting Luz and my *abuela*," said Vicente. "Kate hasn't met them yet."

Fred nodded and tapped on the steering wheel. "Where do you guys live?"

"San Francisco," we said in unison.

Fred chuckled. "Oh, that really is paradise. Especially in the summer. Hope there's not *too* much trouble there."

A photograph on the dashboard caught my eye—a little girl, perhaps five or six, with sandy-colored hair that exactly matched Fred's.

"Is that your daughter?" I asked, glad for an excuse to change the subject.

A huge smile crossed Fred's face. "That's Julie. Picture's from a couple years ago. She's eight now."

"Is she your only child?"

"Yup!" he said. "It's just the two of us. She's my whole world."

Just the two of us? That sweet child didn't have a mother?

As if he could read my thoughts, he added, "My ex-wife ran out on us when Julie was eleven months old. We get a postcard every few months and a phone call once a year or so, but that's about it. She's surfing in Kuta last I heard."

Laurie was eleven months old. My heart broke. I couldn't imagine abandoning Jim and my baby like that. The very thought made me want to run home and scoop Laurie up and hold her close. But I stuffed the thought away—it didn't go with Vicente's stupid cover story.

"Oh, I'm so sorry," I said. "I'm pregnant with twins, and I love the babies so much already."

"Hey, that's great!" Fred exclaimed. "Congrats, you two!"

Irritation flashed through me. Of course he'd conclude Vicente was the father. The very thought made my face warm.

Couldn't Vicente have used any other story?

If we ever went undercover together again, we'd plan this part ahead. Or, even better—*I* would blurt out the embarrassing cover story before he had a chance to. Maybe I'd say I was his court-appointed psychiatrist doing an in-the-field assessment of his sanity.

Or his attorney, making sure he didn't incriminate himself in a pending felony case.

Or his personal doctor, ensuring his continual access to his . . . ahem, *performance* meds for his *difficulties with intimacy.*

The thought brought a genuine smile to my face.

After a few minutes of awkward chitchat in which I very determinedly gave Vicente the cold shoulder, the truck turned onto a long driveway.

"The vineyard and winery." Vicente gestured out the window. Fields of grapevines extended in either direction, and ahead, I could see a couple buildings on a hill. It seemed like there might be a few other outbuildings, but they were hidden among pine trees.

Absolutely beautiful.

A couple minutes later, we pulled up to a lovely Mediterranean-style house.

"Here you are!" said Fred. "Vicente, let me get your cell phone number so I can let you know what the mechanic says."

They exchanged numbers, and then Vicente scooted out of the truck. As I moved to follow him, he reached out to help me out of the cab. I scowled and grabbed a handle instead, carefully jumping to the ground. Pain jolted through my knees on impact, but I trained a defiant expression on Vicente. He shot me a sheepish grin in return.

As Fred's truck pulled away down the driveway, I snapped, "What the heck were you thinking, ambushing me like that?"

"Sorry, *querida*," he replied with a shrug. "Seemed like an explanation that wouldn't raise too many questions. My compliments on your recovery from the surprise. I knew I could count on your theater background. Well, shall we go in and meet Luz?"

"Only if you're not going to make me pretend to be your fiancée."

"Not for Luz," he said slowly. "She knows you're a PI. But if we could keep up the pretense around my *abuela*? Luz doesn't want to worry her. *Abuela* had a heart attack a year ago, and the doctor says she needs to avoid stress, so Luz hasn't told her about the sabotage, or any of the vineyard's troubles."

"You want me to lie to your grandmother about being your fiancée?" I snapped.

"Don't worry. She won't take it too seriously. I've been engaged three times but never made it to the wedding."

"Of course you have," I muttered. "So now I just have to play yet another poor girl caught in the web of Vicente Domingo's so-called charm."

He looked almost wounded, but his eyes twinkled. "When you phrase it that way, you make me sound monstrous."

I shifted my purse to the other shoulder. "Let's just get this case solved so I can go back to being *Mrs.* Kate Connolly. How on earth am I supposed to explain this to my husband?"

He shrugged. "He doesn't seem like the jealous type."

Vicente was right, of course. But that didn't mean I had to like it.

"I am *not* sharing a room with you," I warned.

He raised his hands in surrender. "Of course not. I wouldn't dream of it."

And with that, he knocked on the door.

A moment later, we were greeted by a lovely woman in her thirties, with olive skin and a warm expression. The family resemblance to Vicente was undeniable. Her dark curls spilled around her shoulders, and her eyes were red-rimmed.

"Luz!" Vicente exclaimed. "What's wrong?"

"Vicente!" she replied, barreling into his arms for a hug. "I'm so glad you're here." She pulled back and reached out to shake my hand. "And you must be Kate. Thank you so much for coming. I'm . . . kind of desperate for help, to tell you the truth."

"It's my pleasure, truly. Your brother Gary has gotten me out a lot of jams."

Luz smiled but Vicente looked affronted. "Gary? What about me? I think I've gotten you—"

Luz shoved him before he could finish. "Kate, please, come in."

Vicente held up a hand. "Hang on! You're going to have to introduce Kate to *abuela* as my fiancée. My car broke down on the way here, and that's the cover story we gave to the tow truck driver."

Luz stared at him, then glanced at me. "Please tell me you ran that story by her first."

Vicente shrugged, a gleam in his eye.

Luz smacked his arm, her warmth giving way to exasperation. "*Vicentito!*" she scolded. "*Esta embarazada!*" Though her English was unaccented, she'd switched effortlessly into scolding him in Spanish.

"Yes," I muttered. "It was very embarrassing. Can't believe he didn't have more common sense."

Vicente grinned in my direction. "*Embarazada* means *pregnant*, but it's a common mistake."

Oh. Whoops.

Luz continued, "Are you going to just let *abuela* think that you're going to have a child? She may be resigned to the fact that you're never going to make it to the altar, but she'll be crushed if you tell her she's going to have a great-grandbaby, and it turns out it's all a lie."

He stopped cold, then offered a halfhearted shrug. "Didn't think through that part. I guess we'll just have to tell her it's not my baby."

"Vicente!" Luz and I cried in unison.

Wrinkling his nose, he admitted, "I suppose that won't do, either."

"I don't want to explain anything to *abuela* about what's going on," said Luz, tucking a curl behind her ear. "You know how she worries. And if she has another heart attack because of the stress, I'll never stop blaming myself."

I raised my hands. "How about this . . . what if we tell your *abuela* that I'm a client of Vicente's? Tell her that he brought me up here so I could hide out. A sort of . . . private witness-protection program, if you will. And that we're telling people we're engaged so that no one tries to follow me up from San Francisco."

Luz rested her hand on the doorframe for a moment, then nodded as if satisfied. "It's a good story. *Abuela* will be eager to take you under her wing. She has a soft spot for people in bad situations."

I hoped we'd be able to keep this tangled web of stories straight, but what choice did we have? And all because Vicente hadn't kept his mouth shut.

As if on cue, a crackly, feminine voice called from within the house, "Luz? Who's at the door?"

Luz reached out and touched my arm. "Thank you so much for coming," she whispered. "And for putting up with my insufferable cousin." Then she turned and called, "*Abuela*! Vicente is here!"

With a sharp gasp, a gray-haired woman appeared in the doorway. She was no more than five feet tall, with a face rounded by age. Her eyes sparkled behind her glasses as she exclaimed, "Vicente! It is so good to see you! Come in! You must be hungry. I'll make you a tortilla."

A tortilla? By itself? I wondered.

Vicente kissed his grandmother as we stepped inside. "Abuela, that sounds wonderful."

The old woman paused, her eyes landing on me for the first time. "And who is this lovely girl you've brought home?" she asked Vicente, her gaze darting toward my baby bump in hopeful expectation.

"*Abuela*, this is Kate," he replied. "She's a client of mine. I was worried she wasn't safe in San Francisco, so Luz said I could bring her up here for a few days while things cool off."

The woman gasped and reached out to grab my hands. "You poor thing. I'm Gloria, and we'll take good care of you here. Come, sit down and make yourself at home. I bet you could use a tortilla too."

The house was decorated in sumptuous colors, with paintings of the Spanish countryside gracing the walls. But Luz and Gloria led us through a pair of ornate doors into a simpler sitting area. On the far side of the room, I caught sight of a small kitchen.

Gloria gestured to a sectional couch. "Would you like anything to drink? Water? Wine?"

"Water for me," I replied, gesturing down to my pregnant belly.

"I'll take a red wine," Vicente replied as he sank onto the couch. "Anything that's already open."

Gloria nodded and patted him on the shoulder. "It is so very good to see you, Vicente. I'm glad you thought to bring the poor girl here."

Luz sat next to her cousin, and I chose a seat on the other side of the sectional, facing them. The soft couch cushioned my burdened joints, and I let out a little sigh of relief.

As soon as Gloria bustled off toward the kitchen, I gestured to Luz. "Thank you for the warm welcome. It's beautiful here."

"Wait until you see the rest of the winery," exclaimed Vicente. "My cousin's done an amazing job with the business."

Luz offered a soft smile in return. "I'm trying to," she said. "It's my life's work." Then a serious expression overtook her face. "But it's I who should be thanking you. Did Vicente explain the situation?"

I nodded somberly. "We talked about it in the car on the way up. But you seemed . . . startled when we arrived. Has something else happened?"

"Another note," she whispered. "Let's wait to discuss it. We can go to the wine-tasting cave after you've had something to eat, and we'll be able to talk more freely there. I . . . I was unnerved about everything before. That's why I called Vicente to come help. But after today . . . I'm genuinely afraid."

CHAPTER 3

*A*fraid? Vicente and I glanced at each other, grim expressions on our faces.

But Luz waved her hand. "I'm sorry," she said, regret in her eyes. "I shouldn't have led with that. We'll discuss it in a few minutes."

Gloria emerged from the kitchen carrying a tray, and Luz clamped her mouth shut.

"Water and wine," declared Gloria, setting the tray on the coffee table. Luz visibly flinched, but no one else seemed to notice. A moment later, Gloria disappeared back toward the kitchen.

"So," Luz said, "I understand you've done great work as a PI. Tell me about an interesting case you've solved."

"Well . . ." I reached for a water glass. "The most recent one was a murder on Alcatraz Island."

Her jaw dropped. "At the old prison? What happened?"

"Well, it all started when my brother came to San Francisco on business . . ."

A sizzling sound came from the kitchen, and a delicious smell wafted toward us. I sat up straighter, realizing all at once how hungry I was.

We made small talk about my PI work and Luz's winery for a few minutes, and despite the stress in her eyes, she was an easy conversationalist and a lot of fun to talk to.

How could someone as maddening as Vicente have such charming relatives?

And then Gloria swept into the room carrying two plates, each holding a decadent-looking pastry. "Tortillas!" she cried, handing one plate to me and one to Vicente.

"Thank you!" I breathed.

I bit into the tortilla, then froze, surprised by the savory taste. I'd been wrong. This was definitely not a pastry. "Is this . . . potato?" I asked.

Luz and Vicente laughed aloud, and Gloria slapped her forehead with an open palm.

"Yes, dear," Gloria said. "I should have explained. Spanish tortilla is not like a Mexican tortilla. More like . . . how do you say it . . . an omelet. Egg, potato, very filling. Good for your baby."

"It's delicious!" I replied, shoveling another forkful into my mouth.

Gloria patted my shoulder, a knowing smile on her face. "I can make you another! I was always so hungry when I was pregnant with my babies."

Luz interjected, *"Abuela,* I'm going to steal them off to the wine cave to show them some things, but maybe you can make Kate another tortilla later."

"I would be delighted," I said with a grin as I swallowed the last bite of tortilla. "You're a wonderful cook."

Gloria's eyes sparkled. "Vicente, don't stay away too long. I'm so happy to see you back home."

"I'll be back very soon," he reassured her.

As we slipped out of the room, I took another sip of my water glass. "She's so delightful!" I exclaimed.

"She is," replied Luz warmly. She led us past the paintings of the Spanish countryside and to a back door. "Our parents are still in Spain. Vicente's parents never left, but my mom lived here in Golden for most of her life. She and my father moved back to Spain about five years ago."

"Your mom grew up here?" I gestured at the pine trees. "At the vineyard?"

She led us down a path that curved around the hill. "Yes. *Abuela* came to the United States with our *abuelo* in 1974. They started this vineyard. I came to live with them years ago to learn the trade, and I've taken care of her since *abuelo* passed. I don't want to worry her." She paused to open a door at the bottom of the stairs. "Or disappoint her."

Double wooden doors were set into a rock wall in the hillside. Above it, on top of the hill, was what appeared to be a patio.

"No need to worry about disappointing her, *prima*," Vicente said softly. "She loves you more than anything else in the world."

"That only makes it worse," groaned Luz, unlocking the wooden doors. "Anyway, this is the wine cave."

We walked inside.

The wine cave was somehow both cozy and breathtaking—illuminated by soft track lighting and draped string lights, with tables propped up by old wine barrels. I leaned against one of the tabletops, Vicente at my side and Luz across from us.

"I love this place!" I said.

Luz smiled. "Thank you. We host our weekly wine-tasting events in here. It's beautiful, isn't it? I always come in here when I need time to think."

"I totally understand." I said. After a moment, I drummed my nails against the tabletop and said, "So, Vicente explained what happened with the power outages and the lost grapes, and that you've gotten some odd notes. And then there was a cyberattack, or something?"

Luz nodded grimly. "A break-in, too. Before the cyberattack."

"That's right."

"And something else happened today?" Vicente asked.

She nodded, opening a drawer and pulling out a few pieces of paper. "Another note," she said. "These are the first two, from a few weeks ago."

Vicente and I each reached out to take one, studying the details. The first one I looked at had been typed and printed on basic white paper.

I KNOW WHAT YOU DID. MAYBE ITS TIME TO GIVE UP YOU'RE GRAPES OF WRATH.

"Well," I murmured. "They're referencing a classic novel but made a mistake on the difference between *your* and *you're*."

"I noticed that," said Luz with a dark chuckle. "They missed the apostrophe in *it's*, too."

Vicente and I traded papers, and I read the other note.

HOW ABOUT A MIRACLE? TURN THE WINE INTO WATER.

It was printed on the same type of paper. No spelling errors in this one, I noted—but another allusion, this time to a Bible story. And this one explained why Luz had flinched at Gloria's water-and-wine remark a few minutes earlier. It had been an unwelcome reminder of the strange notes.

Glancing toward Luz, I asked, "And what did they send today?"

Wordlessly, she passed the last piece of paper toward me.

LIGHTS OUT. CLOSE DOWN THE WINERY OR ELSE.

My eyes widened. "They're all disconcerting, but this one reads as a more direct threat. They didn't even bother to try to be clever with a literary reference."

"I know." She ran a hand through her dark hair. "I . . . don't know what to do."

"Let's start thinking through some suspects, so we have a place to begin investigating," I said. "Vicente thought maybe your ex has something to do with it?"

Vicente grumbled his assent.

Luz traced the edge of the table. "It is easier for Vicente to think that Thomas is involved than it is for me. Thomas is many things . . . Vicente always hated him, even when we were all children. Vicente and I spent several summers here together."

"You can say that again," Vicente muttered. "He's a weasel."

She ignored him and continued, "But I have a hard time imagining he would go this far. He wants us to be together. Sometimes he has a terrible way of showing it. But I don't think he wants me to shut down the vineyard or anything."

"Is there anyone who *might* want you to shut down?" I pulled out my trusty legal pad and scribbled a few notes.

"I've thought a lot about it, of course." She paused, pulling down a glass from a shelf and uncorking a bottle of wine. "I'm so sorry, I just need to settle my nerves. As far as other suspects go . . . I did have a manager, Bruce Stringer, whom I fired a few months ago."

"You fired Bruce?" asked Vicente, leaning forward, a new intensity in his eyes. "Why?"

Luz took a sharp breath. "It was after the rolling blackout. We'd decided together to buy grapes from another vineyard, and I told him to mark those barrels of wine. When the wines came of age, we were going to use those bottles to fulfill our contracts, but . . . I was not comfortable pretending the wine was made from our own grapes. But Bruce didn't label the barrels . . ."

Vicente sucked in a sharp breath. "Why didn't you tell me?"

She buried her face in her hands. "Because I was complicit, too, and I didn't want to make excuses for my own behavior. When I confronted Bruce about it, he . . . laughed at me. He told me this wasn't the first time he'd done this . . . that our wine that came of age this year is also mixed, that he'd bought other grapes before. We won an award for this year's wine! It was only a small one, from a local harvest festival. But there's no way to know if the award was for wine made from our grapes or someone else's."

"Oh, Luz," breathed Vicente.

"I was incensed." She took a sip of wine. "I left a message for the head of the committee asking her to call me back. But before she did, I found out that the press release had already been sent out. It was a full story in the local paper and a small item in a couple of national wine magazines."

My heart went out to her.

She raised her head, tears brimming in her eyes. "And I panicked." Her voice squeaked. "A retraction like that would call into question the credibility of my whole operation. No one would trust my label anymore. So, when the head of the committee called me back, I just said that I'd wanted to thank her. I . . . went along with Bruce's deception. And I'm still going along with his deception, because I have no way to distinguish which barrels of wine are really from Castillo's."

"What a mess," Vicente said.

"So, don't you see? It would be a lie to put the blame on Bruce. I hate everything about the situation, but the fault is mine. I own this label, and I was too afraid to come clean and make it right."

Understanding flooded me. "You didn't want to tarnish your grandparents' good name," I said.

Our eyes locked, and she nodded. "Yes. I was afraid of the financial consequences, of course. Afraid that I wouldn't be able to take care of *abuela* as she ages, but more than that . . . I didn't want to ruin her legacy or have to see how disappointed she was in me."

Vicente opened his mouth, then seemed to think better of whatever he'd been about to say.

"So, you fired Bruce after you found out about the award?" I asked.

"Yes," she said, wiping away her tears. "Immediately. He was . . . angry, but I didn't think he seemed angry enough to take revenge, or anything. But with everything that's happened, I'm second-guessing that."

I flipped the page on my notepad. "Were you worried he'd go to the press or sue you or take the dispute public?"

"Not at all." She took a long sip of her wine and chuckled darkly. "He's already gotten a job as a manager at another winery, so he still works in the industry. If the story became public, I'd lose my credibility, but so would he."

"Mutually assured destruction," I murmured.

Vicente began pacing back and forth. "So, if he wanted revenge, he'd have to do it this way—with threats and sabotage, not by publicly shaming you."

"Yes," she whispered. "That's exactly right."

An oppressive silence fell over us.

"Well," I finally said, setting down my pen. "For now at least, Bruce seems like our best suspect. Based on the notes, it seems like the saboteur knows about what happened with the grapes."

"Thomas knows about the grapes, too," said Luz.

Vicente snapped toward her, astonishment on his face. "Why . . . why would you give him that kind of ammunition against you? Luz!"

But she kept her focus on me, refusing to meet his gaze. "I didn't know who to turn to. Thomas and I have a lot of history."

"You can say that again," Vicente muttered.

She took a deep breath. "The day after I fired Bruce, I ran into Thomas in town, and he asked me how I was doing and . . . I burst into tears and the whole story spilled out."

Vicente stalked back toward us. "Why, that no-good weasel, I'll—"

"I'm sorry!" Luz sounded close to tears. "But that doesn't mean he's guilty. I'm not going to date him again—really, I'm not—but just because he's a bad boyfriend doesn't mean he's a criminal."

I held up a hand. "Let's not jump to conclusions until we've done a little more investigating. Both of these men seem like viable suspects. We need a plan of—"

The lights flickered and then went out, plunging us into darkness.

CHAPTER 4

*A*n ear-splitting shriek broke through the blackness, and Luz and I grabbed each other's hands.

"It's okay," we said in unison.

Despite the darkness, I blinked. Luz was trying to reassure me, which meant she hadn't screamed. If Luz hadn't screamed, then . . . I snorted. "Vicente, did you just shriek?"

There was a heavy silence. "No," he muttered in a petulant voice. "You're imagining things."

"It's just a power outage," said Luz, her words steady and calm. "Not the first and not the last, especially around here. Sometimes I think we get a power outage when anyone so much as sneezes on Old Mine Road. We'll head back to the house, and everything will be fine."

Quickly, I sorted through my thoughts. Though I wasn't going to say this to Luz yet—no need to panic her—there was no way this was just a power outage. My mind flitted back to the note.

LIGHTS OUT.

Apparently, the saboteur had meant that literally.

A beam of light appeared, dancing in the darkness and then wobbling toward the doorway—Luz had flicked on her cell phone's flashlight. "Let's go," she said.

I followed her toward the door. "Stay alert," I added in a low voice. "Just in case."

When she opened the door, the harsh blackness relinquished its hold—though we hadn't been in the dark for long, I closed my eyes for a moment against the sun's sharp light. We headed up the hill, my body tense as I listened for anything suspicious. I half-expected an attacker to jump out from behind the nearest pine tree.

But everything lay calm and quiet as we reached the back door and entered the still house. Though it was somewhat dim inside, the windows gave enough light to see by.

"That was unsettling," murmured Luz.

I shifted my weight from foot to foot and gazed around the room. "Very."

"I'll check on *abuela*," said Luz. "Make sure she's all right and has everything she needs."

She left Vicente and me alone, and I leaned against the beige wall.

"So, what do you think?" I asked quietly. "About the outage?"

He furrowed his brow. "Too much of a coincidence, don't you think? A power outage after a note like that?"

That confirmed my instincts. "I was thinking the same thing."

He whipped out his phone and tapped a few times on the screen. "I'll check the power company's website to confirm that theory. If it's a widespread outage, with other neighbors affected . . . well, I've seen crazier coincidences a time or two in my years as a PI. But if it's not a widespread outage, I want to go investigate the property. Can you stay here with my *abuela* and Luz?"

"Shouldn't we go together?" I asked, pursing my lips. "For safety?"

He clenched his jaw. "It'll give you some time to discuss the case with Luz. You can ask her more questions and see if she can think of anything else. Plus, you'll keep an eye and ear out to make sure this sabotaging freak doesn't escalate this sick little game."

It still seemed like splitting up was risky. What wasn't he telling me? "Are you worried about Luz being attacked? Is that why you want me to stay here?"

He sighed, his mouth set in a grim line. "I don't know what's going on, but I don't like it. I'd do anything to keep Luz and my *abuela* safe. I love them . . . but it's more than that. I owe them." Then he tilted the phone screen toward me, showing the power company's website. "No outages." After a long pause, he added, "I feel like this is my fault."

I furrowed my brow. "What do you mean by *you owe them* and *you feel like it's your fault?*"

He let out a sigh. "*Abuelo* always wanted Luz and her brother, Gary, and me to run the vineyard together—a real family business—but I wasn't interested. Obviously, neither was Gary because he went off to law school. But I wanted to make my own way, and so I became a private investigator."

I didn't reply, waiting for him to continue.

"If Luz and I were working together, she never would have needed to hire a manager." He gestured wildly with his hands. "The two of us together could have handled the work of running the vineyard. My grandparents always did it together—they didn't need to hire managers. But it's just too much for one person."

The realization dawned on me all at once. Vicente felt guilty for leaving the family business and choosing another career. I hadn't seen that sort of vulnerability from him before, and it made me feel more charitably toward him.

"It's not your fault that she's in this mess, you know," I murmured, scuffing my foot against the floor.

"Feels like it. If she hadn't hired Bruce . . ." He let out a long, loud sigh. "I know we can't live life worrying about the ways things might have turned out differently. But on this, I can't help but wonder."

I tried to imagine Vicente as a rural grape farmer in small-town Golden, inspecting the harvest in his black jeans and leather jacket, hauling supplies from the feed store on the back of his motorcycle. The image brought a smirk to my face, and I turned away to school my features into an expression of serious contemplation.

"There's no telling how things might have turned out if we'd made different choices," I replied finally. "Things might be different at the vineyard, but you might have been a terrible winery owner."

He snorted. "Maybe I was always afraid of failing at the family business."

"And," I continued, "you've done a lot of good as a PI. You've caught criminals and proven the innocence of people who might have otherwise ended up behind bars."

"I know, I know. Still, this is my family."

There was a long pause.

"Well," I said slowly. "We have two good suspects. One way or another, we'll figure out who's responsible for the sabotage."

A few minutes later, Luz returned. "*Abuela* is just fine. She thinks the power company needs to get their act together."

"She's not wrong about that," said Vicente, "but ..."

"But this has to be another act of sabotage," finished Luz. "Too much of a coincidence."

"Well, that makes three of us," I said. "It's unanimous. Something's not right about this blackout." I fanned myself with my notepad. Despite the wine cave being naturally cooler than the main house, without the air conditioning running, it was already getting hot.

Vicente nodded. "I'm going to have a look around the property. I want you and Kate to stay here where it's safe."

Luz shook her head. "It's *my* vineyard, Chente. I'm not going to hide in the house if something's going on."

"Do it for *abuela*," he replied. "Someone has to stay here to keep an eye on her."

For a second, she hesitated, then nodded. "Fine, then. Kate and I will stay."

Vicente pulled his cousin into a brief hug. "I'll try to be quick about it."

Then he glided out the door with catlike stealth. We watched him go, then headed into the living room and sank into a pair of stuffed chairs. For a full minute, silence hovered over us.

Finally, I said, "Let's talk about the case a little more, since we got interrupted by the power outage. We have two solid suspects. Is there anyone else at all?"

Luz paused, tilting her head back and forth. "Well . . . I also have wondered a time or two if Bruce's wife might be involved. To tell you the truth, that suspicion is why I agreed to stay here with *abuela* instead of checking out the vineyard with Vicente. I can't imagine

Bruce or Thomas hurting *abuela*, but Regina . . . I don't understand her, and I'm not sure I can predict her behavior."

"Regina is Bruce's wife?" I asked, flipping a page in my notepad.

"Yes." She pulled an elastic off her wrist and started to braid her dark hair. "It's probably nothing, of course . . ."

When she didn't continue, I offered, "I've been doing this long enough to know that when someone says *it's probably nothing*, it's usually a lead worth following up on."

That seemed to set her at ease. She finished the braid and pressed her palms together. "Bruce was angry when I fired him, but like I said earlier, it didn't seem as if he was angry enough to want revenge, or anything like that. He got another job right away, so it didn't hurt them financially. In our last conversation, it even seemed that he understood why I had to fire him. But Regina"—she chuckled and rolled her eyes—"Regina is another story altogether. She left three or four voicemail messages over the last couple weeks."

Interesting. "What kind of messages?"

"Oh, she was absolutely livid." She hesitated, thinking. "She said that I'd betrayed Bruce—that it was his creativity that had saved the wine harvest and our contracts, and that I was punishing him for it."

I smirked. "*Creativity*, huh? That's certainly one word for it."

She threw her hands in the air. "Even though Bruce and I agreed together to buy the grapes! Bruce's *only* unique contribution to this mess was failing to label the barrels!" Luz fiddled with a ring on her right hand and made a face. "Regina's always been a little volatile, though. Three years ago, she thought Bruce and I were having an affair."

Very, very interesting. "An affair? Why'd she think that?"

"We'd had a weaker harvest—that turned out to be the year Bruce bought another vineyard's grapes behind my back. He was working longer hours—we both were. I guess she got suspicious."

"What happened? Did she confront him?"

She raised her eyebrows. "No, she confronted *me*. Called me one evening while we were working on the books."

I grimaced. "Yikes."

"Yeah. *Abuela* was with us and everything when we were working late that week—back then, she'd help out occasionally when we were extra busy. So it wasn't like an affair was even possible, even if I *were* attracted to Bruce or was the sort of person who'd sleep with an employee." She let out a sigh. "Which I'm not. Anyway, Regina screamed at me for what felt like a solid minute, though to tell you the truth, it was probably only like fifteen seconds before I put her on speakerphone. Bruce went home right away to talk to her. From what I understand, he gave her his phone and showed her all our messages, and she was satisfied that there was nothing unprofessional in any of them."

I drummed my fingers against my notepad. "So she has a history of jumping to conclusions and lashing out."

"Yeah . . ." Luz locked eyes with me for a long moment, then glanced down at her lap. "She did snub me last time I went into town, too—we passed each other in the produce section at the grocery store. Even though I felt awkward, I smiled and waved, but she flat-out turned her back on me. But like I said, it's probably nothing. I mean, she definitely has a temper and she's unpredictable, but I . . . I think she's just petty. I don't know that she's ever escalated beyond screaming phone calls."

"Still," I said, "it's a reasonable lead worth investigating. Even if it turns out to be nothing, we don't want to leave any stones unturned."

My stomach gurgled audibly.

"Oh!" Luz exclaimed. "Are you hungry?"

I chuckled, resting a hand on my belly. "I practically just ate, but it does seem like the twins are always hungry. Although I ate a lot during my first pregnancy, too, and that was just one baby."

She stood. "*Abuela* will whip up more food for you. Let's go back to the kitchen—we'll do tapas and virgin sangria."

"But the power's out," I said, struggling to extricate myself from the stuffed chair. "We can't cook anything."

Luz grinned and helped me to my feet. "Doesn't matter. We have a gas stove, so as long as we haven't lost the lighter, *abuela* can make tapas on the stovetop."

An hour and a half later, I leaned back against the couch cushions, stuffed to the brim. The food had been delicious—as had the mocktail. Gloria was spoiling me, and I didn't mind it one bit.

Gloria hovered over me with a motherly air. "I can make more tapas!" she exclaimed. "What did you like best? The *croquetas*? Tortillas? *Patatas bravas*?"

"I can't eat another bite," I replied with a contented groan. "Your cooking is so good that I ate more than I should have already!"

"Babies need food." She crossed her arms. "I will make another tortilla for you."

"*Abuela!*" chided Luz. "Kate says she's full."

Gloria leveled a suspicious gaze at me, as if she couldn't quite believe it, then nodded and sat next to Luz on the sectional. "Where is Vicente?" she asked. "How long can a phone call take?"

I'd been wondering the same thing—and from the grimace that crossed Luz's face, I suspected I wasn't alone. We'd told Gloria that he'd stepped out to take a call . . . and now we needed to invent another excuse.

Abuela had a heart attack a year ago, Vicente had said. *She needs to avoid stress.*

Well, I certainly wouldn't be responsible for killing Vicente's grandmother.

"Oh, he sent me a message that he went to run an errand," I said smoothly. "He'll be back soon."

He should have returned by now—hadn't he just popped outside to look around? But the vineyard was large. *He's probably just combing through things carefully—maybe taking photos of anything that looks like potential evidence.*

Still, I felt vaguely sick to my stomach. I shouldn't have let him go alone.

Where are you, Vicente?

CHAPTER 5

*T*he doorbell chimed its melodious tune.

Vicente must be back! I let out a little sigh of relief, the guilt receding. It was true—I shouldn't have let him go alone.

Mistakes were made, but all's well that ends well. The babies shimmied in my abdomen, sending a fluttering feeling through me.

Luz shot to her feet. "There he is! I'll let him in."

"I'll come, too," I replied, pushing myself upward with a grunt and flailing to catch my balance. Vicente and I would need to steal away to discuss the case and go over any evidence he'd collected.

Hopefully, he'd made a break in the investigation while he was away.

We left Gloria in the kitchen and headed for the entryway. As we walked toward the door, I glanced out the large front windows.

Oh no. My heart sank. Fred's tow truck was parked in the driveway. Which meant . . .

Vicente's not back. Where could he be?

Luz threw open the door. "Oh!" she said, surprise lacing her voice. "Hey, Fred."

The tow truck driver stood on the doorstep, an apologetic expression on his face. "Hey, Luz! Sorry to just show up like this. I heard back from the mechanic."

"Oh," she said again, offering a shy smile.

His face blushed pink. "Tried to call Vicente, but it went straight to voicemail, so I figured I might as well swing back here and let ya know. Since I didn't have any more calls about cars needing towing. Vicente around?"

It went straight to voicemail. Something churned in my stomach. Did that mean Vicente's phone was off? Or just that he'd declined the call right away, before it could start ringing?

But why would he decline a call? Was he in some sort of danger and couldn't let his phone make noise?

I bit down hard on my tongue. I was letting my mind run away with me.

For a second, I thought that detail would jar Luz out of her composure, but she recovered herself. "Um, Vicente's not here right now. But, thanks so much. Would you mind coming in? We've had a power outage, and I don't want to let out too much air conditioning."

"Sure!" he said enthusiastically.

Huh. If I didn't know any better, I might think sparks were flying between Fred and Luz. They'd make a cute couple, I decided.

"Power outage, huh?" he asked as she closed the door. "Is a line down, or are they doing another rolling blackout?"

"Neither. It's just us," said Luz. "Thankfully, we're done processing the season's wine, so the worst part is the loss of air conditioning."

He tilted his head. "Just you guys? Only the house, or the whole winery?"

"The wine cave's out, too, so not just the house."

His brows furrowed. "That's funny. Mind if I take a look at your breaker?"

"Uh, sure," she said. "I'd really appreciate that. It's in the barn. Fastest way is out the back door. Let's go this way."

The three of us headed down the hall, and Luz said, "What did the mechanic say about Vicente's car?"

"Right! Mechanic!" exclaimed Fred, running a hand over his clean-shaven face. "Whole reason I came here. Anyway, it's a simple fix, but because it's a fancy car, he has to get a part in from Sacramento. It'll be here by ten o'clock in the morning, and the car should be good to go by tomorrow evening."

"That's great news." Luz reached up to smooth her braid as we walked.

We turned the corner and pushed through the back door into the sweltering heat. I would *definitely* need a freezing shower after this.

But the barn was in sight—in the opposite direction of the wine cave—so I just waddled faster, trying my best to keep up with Luz and Fred.

"Is everything all right, Luz?" Fred asked. "You seem . . . tense."

She chuckled and shoved her hands in her pockets. "Are any of the vineyard owners all right this year? Everyone's on edge with the power shortages and the drought."

"Fair enough," he replied slowly.

From my vantage point behind them, I caught him giving her a sideways look, as if he didn't quite believe her.

Luz unlocked a side door, and we strolled into the barn. I braced myself for the scent of hay and manure, but instead the air smelled vaguely of . . .

Wine.

It only took me a second to realize why. My gaze traced the architecture—the barn had originally been built to house horses, but it had since been converted into a small wine processing plant. Barrels of wine occupied the stalls, and fermenting tanks were evenly spaced all the way down the central walkway.

Luz turned to the right and gestured to a panel box. "Breaker is there," she said.

Fred brushed past her and opened the box. I tried to make eye contact with Luz, but she was staring off into space, a trace of a smile on her lips.

Not imagining the chemistry. They'd definitely be a cute couple.

"That's odd," Fred muttered.

There was a series of loud *clicks* from the direction of the box.

Is he flipping the breakers?

"What is it?" Luz asked, popping up onto her tiptoes and peering toward him.

"Your main circuit breaker tripped," said Fred, wiping his forehead with the back of his arm. "The big central one. You don't see that very often—usually it's just individual breakers that trip. If it happens again, have an electrician come look at it."

"Can you fix it for now?" she asked.

"Yep," he said. "I'm flipping off all the individual circuit breakers first. Then I'll turn the main power back on, and then reset the individual breakers. Safer that way. Don't want to risk frying myself."

"I don't know, *Fried Fred* has a lilt to it," she teased.

He turned his head and rolled his eyes at her, but he was smiling.

I'd left my notepad in the house, so I fanned myself with my hand. "What would cause a main circuit breaker to flip?"

He flipped a few more breakers. "Mmm. Maybe a power surge from the electric company, but I doubt that was it. If that were the case, Castillo's probably wouldn't be the only customer affected. There's not a cloud in the sky, so it wasn't a lightning strike. Luz, have you plugged in anything new that might take a lot of power?"

"No," she murmured, clenching her fists at her sides.

He clicked a few more breakers, and the whole atmosphere changed. The lights flicked on, and the gentle rumble of an air conditioning unit roared to life.

Luz jolted, glancing first at Fred, then at me. "That's it?"

"Yeah," he said. "But really do call an electrician if it happens again, in case there's a short circuit in the panel."

This really, truly can't be a coincidence. The saboteur had been here . . . had flipped the circuit breaker to shut off the power. I was sure of it.

My mind flickered back to the morning's ominous note. *LIGHTS OUT.*

But why cut the power? And why hadn't Vicente returned?

A sick feeling squirmed in my stomach. Had the saboteur killed the power to lure Luz out of the house? Had they hurt Vicente?

Don't panic, I warned myself. *There's probably a perfectly good explanation for why Vicente's not back.*

But another detail churned in my mind—that Fred had said he'd tried to call Vicente, but his phone had gone to voicemail.

Why was Vicente not answering his phone?

"Well, thanks so much for your help," said Luz. "Shall we head back to the house?"

Fred's phone rang, and he tipped his hat. "Sounds like I have a call coming in. I'd best be off." He answered the phone. "Golden Medal Tow Service. How can I help you?" He listened for a second, then nodded at us and whispered, "I've got a job. Talk to you ladies later."

He strode out of the barn, and I turned to Luz.

"Well, what do you think?" I asked.

She crossed her arms. "About the power outage?"

I gave a small nod.

Hissing through her teeth, she said, "Do you think someone plugged in something in one of the outbuildings? Something that used so much power it overwhelmed the system?"

Hadn't thought of that. "That's possible," I replied. "But I was thinking that they might have manually flipped the breaker."

She looked around the barn. "This building stays locked," she said. Sweat beaded on her brow. "To keep the machinery safe."

"Let's look around for any sign of forced entry, then. That will help us narrow down what happened."

I walked along the exterior wall, checking the windows, and Luz headed to the other end of the barn. A little gray tabby materialized out of nowhere and rubbed against my legs.

"Hi, sweet girl," I murmured, squatting down and scratching her chin. She mewed at me, then wandered off. I grabbed the wooden framing to haul myself back to my feet.

Was I out of breath from *petting a cat*? This pregnancy was getting ridiculous.

"Found it!" called Luz.

I hobbled in the direction of her voice. She was standing at a door on the other side of the barn. A shattered window was set in the doorway, and broken glass littered the floor in front of her.

"Be careful!" I called.

She glanced down at the shards of glass and took a step back.

I caught up with her and studied the scene. "Window was broken from the outside," I said. "That's why the glass sprayed inward. Then the burglar just reached through and unlocked the door."

"All that trouble to knock out the power?" she asked slowly, turning and eyeing the machinery with a groan. "Man, I'm going to have to get a technician out here to inspect the equipment. Make sure that they didn't sabotage it."

I took pictures of the door with my phone camera, then drifted away to look through the barn for any other clues. Nothing looked out of place.

"I'm worried about Vicente," she called. "Whoever knocked out the power was here . . . that meant they were still nearby when he went to investigate."

My jaw tightened, and I turned back toward her. "It concerns me that he's not answering his phone, too. Now, there are a lot of reasonable explanations. No need to panic yet. He could be gathering evidence, and he might not want to answer his phone if he's suspicious that the saboteur is on the property."

"Let's get the golf cart." Luz squared her shoulders. "We need to find my cousin *now*."

CHAPTER 6

*L*uz and I spent forty minutes driving through the vineyard, calling for Vicente. But there was no sign of him.

"Where could he be?" she demanded, her voice cracking. She slammed her hand against the steering wheel and scrunched up her face, fighting off tears. "We've looked everywhere."

"I don't like it," I said. "I don't like it at all. But let's remember that there are a lot of reasonable explanations. Sabotage is one thing, violence is another—it would be a huge escalation for someone to hurt or kidnap Vicente. We need to stay calm and keep our heads clear."

But Luz wasn't calm. Not even close. "Should we file a missing-person report?" Her breaths were coming fast and shallow. "Oh my gosh. What will I tell *abuela* if something's happened to him?"

I swallowed back a wave of nausea. "There's no point in filing a report yet. He's an adult, and he hasn't been missing twenty-four hours. That means police won't take it seriously. They might let you file a report if you disclosed everything—the sabotage, the notes . . . all the reasons you're concerned for his safety—but they're still not going to start looking for him until tomorrow. Plus"—I hesitated—"police reports are generally something the public can request, and could be used in, say, a news story."

She looked almost green as she pulled out her phone. "But surely we have to try." Then she swore under her breath. "No cell service here. Let's go back to the house. Maybe he's come home. If not, we can call from there."

She shoved her phone back in her pocket and hit the gas pedal, still breathing too quickly. I put my hand on her shoulder, hoping to calm her panic attack. The wheels of the golf cart churned on the gravel path, spitting pebbles out behind it. Then we were gliding forward, back toward the blessed air conditioning.

Please, let Vicente be there, safe and sound, I prayed.

When we arrived back at the house, Luz ran inside. I headed after her, but quickly despaired of keeping up. I was not in any kind of shape to run.

"*Abuela!*" she called as she opened the door.

I ambled inside, huffing and puffing and muttering, "I'm ready to not be pregnant anymore."

Luz met me when I was halfway to the kitchen. "*Abuela* says he's not home yet," she whispered. "I acted unconcerned in front of her, but I'm really, really starting to freak out."

The fear was apparent on Luz's face, and I swallowed back my worry that she hadn't acted nearly as unconcerned as she thought.

"I have an idea," I said, trying to project calm control. "One that might help us find Vicente faster than the police will."

"Shoot."

"Let's invite the suspects here. I'll ask them questions, and we'll see if we can narrow down the identity of our saboteur—and if we can glean anything that will help us figure out where your cousin is."

She sucked in a sharp breath. "Is that safe? What if we corner the culprit, and . . ."

"Take deep breaths. Nothing about this situation is safe," I replied evenly. "The best thing we can do is catch the saboteur as quickly as possible, before the situation escalates further."

For a moment, she seemed to consider this. Then, her shoulders slumped, and she gave in. "Vicente said you're the best PI he knows."

My chest puffed up a little at the compliment. *He said that? Really?* He'd never deign to say such a thing to my face.

She continued. "I trust his judgment, and so I trust you. Let's do it."

"Then call Thomas and Bruce and ask if they can meet us here. Have Bruce bring his wife."

Luz pulled out her phone and started making calls. I snatched my notepad from the living room and studied my scribbles, reminding myself of everything I knew about the case. I wanted to go into these interrogations as prepared as I possibly could be.

Seven minutes later, a knock sounded at the door. I tilted my head as Luz hurried to answer it.

That was fast. Town was ten minutes away—I'd mapped the distance earlier. Had the new arrival been on the road already—or had they been hanging out nearby? *Doesn't necessarily mean anything, but it's potentially suspicious,* I concluded. Something to follow up on.

"Thank you so much for coming," said Luz.

"Well," barked a shrill, headache-inducing voice. "I want to know why you dragged us all the way out here. To gloat about how you fired my husband, because you're a smug traitor?"

"Now, Regina," chided a man who could only be Bruce, Luz's former manager. "That's unkind."

While Regina was openly aggressive, there was something in Bruce's tone I didn't like. He seemed . . . oily. Outwardly polite, but snakelike.

"Let's talk more in the wine cave," said Luz, glancing toward the hallway that led to the kitchen.

"Why?" spat Regina. She was a tall brunette with frown lines around her mouth and a stiff posture. Her husband, in contrast, was short for a man—they were almost exactly equal in height—with a more relaxed demeanor.

I stood and crossed the room toward them—they smelled vaguely of cigarette smoke, and my nose twitched. "I'm Kate Connolly, a private investigator looking into some odd happenings here at the vineyard. I'd like to ask you a few questions."

Regina blinked several times at me. "You're a PI? I thought Vicente had brought a fiancée to town."

I stared her down coldly. "Rumors of our engagement have been greatly exaggerated."

If Vicente weren't missing, I'd have stuck with the cover story. But if the saboteur had abducted Vicente, there wasn't time to be coy or indirect.

She crossed her arms. "So, what's the problem?"

"Like Luz said, we'll talk in the wine cave." I glanced at Luz. "Has Thomas replied?"

Glancing at her phone, Luz said, "Yeah, he's finishing up something at the store and will head this way soon."

"Thomas?" asked Bruce. "Why's he coming? What's this about?"

I jerked my head toward the back door. "Let's go."

In strained silence, we made our way to the wine cave. When we went inside, Bruce let out a chuckle.

"Still feels like home," he said, craning his neck to look around the room.

"Of course it does," retorted his wife. "You gave the best years of your life to this place, before *she* threw you out like trash."

Luz's head jerked up. "Now, wait just a minute—"

"Stop!" I held up a hand. "No bickering, please."

But Regina leaned against the bar and snapped, "Bruce *saved* Castillo's. Don't you get that?" She jabbed a finger in Luz's direction. "Because he's able to think outside the box and problem-solve creatively, and you're not." For the first time, I noticed her nails—painted an obnoxious neon green. My friend Paula could pull that shade off, but on Regina, the incandescent polish looked out of place.

I sat down on a wine-barrel chair and offered Regina an easy smile. "So, it made you angry when Luz fired Bruce?"

"Of course it did!" She scowled at me.

"Angry enough to take revenge?" I asked evenly, pressing my fingertips together.

She fell silent, her brow furrowing.

"What's that supposed to mean?" demanded Bruce.

"It's just a question."

"What kind of revenge are you talking about?" Concern lines creased Bruce's forehead. "What's going on?"

For now, I'd keep my cards hidden, in hopes that they'd slip up and reveal that they knew something. "We were hoping you might be able to tell us."

"I need a drink," he muttered, crossing around the bar to the line of wine bottles. He popped a cork and poured himself a full glass of red.

It's like he thinks he's still the manager here.

For a second, Luz seemed startled by his sense of entitlement, too. We made eye contact, and she shrugged.

So he's entitled. Lots of people are entitled, of course, but it's not a mark in his favor.

He took a sip of the wine, closed his eyes, and let out a satisfied sigh. "That's better. Now, what on earth is going on?"

"Vicente's missing." The words exploded out of Luz's mouth. She hesitated, as if wondering if she'd said too much.

Bruce almost dropped the wine glass, his eyes widening. "What do you mean, *missing*? Like, from here? Or is he in San Francisco still?"

I intervened. "Have either of you sent any threatening notes to Luz?"

Bruce shook his head adamantly, then glanced at his wife in silent question. "Hon, you haven't threatened Luz, have you?"

She gasped and wheeled on him. "What are you accusing me of, Bruce? How dare you!"

He took another sip of wine and muttered, "You have no qualms about accusing me of having an affair, so maybe we're even now."

I jotted down a few notes about their argument. *Quick to accuse each other. Maybe a rocky marriage. B seems to think R capable of threatening notes.*

"*Hmmph!*" She stared him down imperiously. "Well, in answer to your *deeply hurtful* question, no, I have not threatened your traitorous ex-boss in any way. I don't know anything about any notes, threatening or otherwise, or about where her stupid brother is."

"Cousin," said Luz through gritted teeth.

Bruce's cheek twitched, and he turned to Luz. "Things ended badly with my job here, but . . . this sounds serious. Can you start from the beginning? Maybe I can help."

The door to the wine cave swung open on creaking hinges.

CHAPTER 7

*G*loria appeared in the doorway to the wine cave, silhouetted against the outdoor light.

Luz stood abruptly. "*Abuela*? Is everything all right?"

The old woman stepped into the cave. "I was just coming to see if . . . oh! Bruce!" Her face lit up. "It's so good to see you! I've missed you around here."

"*Abuela!*" Bruce exclaimed. He set down his wine and hurried across the room to give the old woman a hug. "Still spry as ever, I see."

When he released her, she grinned at me. "This one here is my honorary grandson. I was very sad when he got a better offer from another vineyard, but I understood—strapping young men have to prioritize their careers, you know."

I almost chuckled at the characterization of Bruce as *a strapping young man*—he was about fifty, with a considerable paunch beneath his plaid button-up—but from Gloria's standpoint, I supposed we were all pretty young.

Gloria sniffed the air. "Bruce, you started smoking again?" she asked. "I smell cigarettes on you."

He shifted sheepishly from foot to foot. "Well, you know, stress of a new job and all."

She crossed her arms. "Those things will kill you, you know."

He waved his hand. "I know. You talked me into quitting last time. I'll quit again soon. Promise." Then a look of concern crossed his face. "What brought you down here, *abuela*?"

I watched Regina out of the corner of my eye. She'd fallen silent, a sour expression on her face, but was pouring herself a glass of wine.

"Well," said Gloria. "The lights came back on, but the air conditioning in the house didn't, and it was getting too hot. I came to see if we needed to call an electrician. But it seems like there's air conditioning down here."

Luz nodded quickly. "Oh, I wonder if it got damaged when we flipped the breakers. I'll call a technician to take care of it right away. We can't be without AC in there."

"It probably just needs to be reset," said Bruce, waving a hand. "I'll take a look at it. If that doesn't work, you can call someone."

Gloria looped her arm through his. "I'll come with you. We haven't had a chance to have one of our visits since you took that new job. Oh! And you must stay for a tortilla, and tell me about why you're stressed."

"I wouldn't dream of turning down one of your tortillas, *abuela*," he replied. "And I really will quit smoking. Soon."

I drew close to Luz with a questioning expression, but she just nodded at me.

"He wouldn't hurt her," she whispered. "I can't vouch for what else he might do, but he genuinely loves *abuela*."

Bruce and Gloria disappeared out the door.

In a soft murmur, I replied, "But when you asked if it was safe to have them come . . . ?"

Then her eyes jerked to Regina, and I understood. Luz hadn't been worried about Gloria's safety around Bruce—which echoed what she'd said earlier. But she wasn't as certain about Bruce's wife.

Good to know.

Luz's phone buzzed, and she let out a sigh. "Thomas just texted me —he's at the house. I'll bring him down."

She headed toward the door, leaving Regina and me awkwardly sizing each other up. For her part, Regina pointedly ignored me.

"So," I said, breaking the silence. "Did you or Bruce tell anyone about the . . . reasons for Bruce's departure from Castillo's? Gloria seemed to think he'd gotten a better offer somewhere else and left of his own accord, so I've gathered the whole thing was kept hush-hush."

"Gloria's a foolish old woman," muttered Regina, tapping her neon-green nails on the countertop. "I don't know why Bruce is so fond of her."

"You could try answering my questions instead of avoiding them." I leaned forward, trying to meet her gaze, but she wouldn't look at me. "As I said, I'm a private investigator. That means I'm working for someone—Luz hired me—but it doesn't mean that I'm interested in anything except the truth."

She finally looked at me, something like surprise in her expression.

I pushed my advantage. "I just want the truth, Regina. I want to know who's been sending threats to Luz and what happened to Vicente."

She sank onto the wine-barrel seat and studied me. "This isn't a setup?"

"Why would it be a setup?" I started scrawling on my notepad.

"I don't know," she muttered, cracking her neck. "Just seemed weird for Luz to haul us out here like this."

"Her cousin is missing," I reminded her.

She seemed to sink into thought for a moment, then shot to her feet, glowering. "Why would she think we had anything to do with that? Hasn't Bruce suffered enough? Haven't *I* suffered enough?"

Continues to deflect, I wrote on my legal pad.

"My husband gave that traitor the best years of his life and career!" With each sentence, she grew louder.

The door opened, and Luz walked back in, followed by a handsome man whose sandy hair fell nearly to his shoulders. His chin was dotted with stubble, and even in the soft light of the wine cave, his piercing blue eyes caught my attention.

This must be the ex-boyfriend. "Thomas?" I asked.

"That's me," he said, nodding back at me. "Nice to meet you, Detective Connolly."

Detective Connolly. I rather liked the sound of that . . . but I was a PI, not a detective. Wouldn't do to inflate my credentials. "Just call me Kate," I said with a smile.

But Regina wasn't done ranting. She wheeled on Luz and stamped her foot. "You make me sick! I can't believe you'd have the audacity to drag us out here and level these accusations at us, after all we did for you!"

Luz drew back, tucking a strand of loose hair behind her ear. "Excuse me?" she asked icily.

"You're a traitor!" Regina thundered. "When are you going to wake up and offer my husband his job back? You—"

"Now, wait just a minute," Thomas interjected, stalking forward to insert himself between the two women. His eyes glinted in the soft light. "You can't just stand there and yell at her like that. Bruce deserved to get fired. He was unethical and insubordinate. You're lucky I'm willing to do business with the winery that hired him."

Regina stopped short, her mouth hanging open. After a long pause, she snapped back to Luz. "So, you've been spreading the story all over town, I see? It wasn't enough to fire Bruce or to accuse him of heaven knows what—you're trying to start rumors that will get him fired from his new job, too?"

"If you're so convinced he did nothing wrong," said Luz dryly. "Then why are you worried the story would get him fired?"

Regina glared at her.

"But," continued Luz, taking a step back and leaning against the bar, "in answer to your question—no, I'm not interested in spreading the story, and I haven't talked about it to many people. I ran into Thomas shortly after I fired Bruce. I wasn't myself, and he could tell something was wrong. He wouldn't let it go. So, I finally told him what had happened, and, like a good friend, he helped me process it."

Thomas smiled gently, not seeming to notice her pointed use of the word *friend*. "I'll always be here for you, my light and love."

Luz ignored him.

It was a cheesy line that might have been cute if I didn't know their history. *This guy just won't take no for an answer, will he?*

Which, of course, didn't necessarily mean he was the saboteur, but it did make me a little more suspicious of him. But Regina's reaction was even more over the top. Everywhere I looked, there was another red flag.

My chest tightened with worry. How long had Vicente been missing? I glanced at my phone to check the time. It was 3:32, which meant . . . four hours and eleven minutes since the power outage.

Definitely too long. But not *so* long that there couldn't be a reasonable explanation. Cell service was spotty here. He might have found a good clue and gone off to follow a lead. Maybe he'd tried to send an explanatory text message, but it hadn't gone through.

But this heat was unrelenting.

What if he'd gotten sunstroke and was passed out somewhere?

I quickly gathered my thoughts. "Thomas, some odd things have been happening here at the vineyard. We brought you here to ask you a few questions."

"Right," he said, pulling up a wine-barrel chair to face me. "How can I help? What's going on?"

Briefly, I explained the history of sabotage, watching Thomas's face for his reactions. When I described the notes, he seemed concerned. That concern was replaced by alarm when I mentioned the break-in, and by disgust at the cyberattack. By the time I got to the events of the day, he rounded on Regina.

"You expect us to think you and Bruce weren't behind this?" he demanded. "You're the only ones who have a bone to pick with Luz." He looked around the wine cave. "Where is Bruce, anyway?"

"*Abuela* stole him away," said Luz. "He's helping her reset the air conditioning in the apartment—it didn't come on when we got the power back."

Thomas looked at her, aghast. "What if he hurts her?"

Regina openly rolled her eyes. "Bruce and I didn't do any of this crap, but even if we did, Gloria's basically his grandmother. He'd sooner chew off his own leg than harm a hair on her stupid gray head."

Luz's jaw tightened.

I interjected before she could lash out at Regina. "We're not accusing anyone here. I just want to gather information. Could—"

Regina cut me off and pointed a finger. "It was probably Thomas."

He blinked at her several times, his blue eyes taking on an even icier glint. "What . . . are you talking about? Why would I do something like this?"

"Oh, please." Regina took a long slurp of wine. "Everyone knows you're bitter that Luz dumped you. Not to mention that she's your biggest competition for catering contracts. You happened to run into her after she traitorously fired my husband, and she couldn't help but cry in your arms, right? So you saw an opportunity—make it look like Bruce and I were tormenting her so that she'd come to you for comfort."

Thomas's face reddened. "You have a lot of nerve—"

"And if that didn't work," Regina spat, "you *still* stood to gain from it. If she's driven out of business, you'll make a lot of money catering events that would have been held here at Castillo's."

"I would never hurt Luz!" he yelled.

"Tell me about the breakup," I said before Regina could reply.

He opened and closed his mouth. A moth fluttered around the string of lights that hung above his head. Finally, he said, "She . . . we broke up ten months ago. We've been on-again, off-again since high school."

"Mostly off-again," Luz said. "We've dated three times—the first time for a month during our senior year at Golden High, the second time for four months right after college, and this last time for about a year."

"Thirteen months and five days." He ran a hand through his hair.

She rolled her eyes.

"Why'd you break up?" I asked.

"I ended things for good," said Luz, "after he cheated on me."

Thomas looked stricken. "It was a meaningless one-night stand, babe. I've told you over and over again—"

"I won't be made a fool of." Luz's face hardened to steel. "Not again. And I'm not the first or second or third woman you've done this to. I should have known better than to try to change you."

"I swear I'm different now. I've never felt this way about anyone before. I love you!"

"Should have thought of that before you unzipped your pants," Luz muttered. "Thomas, you have to move on. You're not going to have another chance with me. Ever. Third time was the charm, and you ruined it."

He fell silent.

I pursed my lips. "Okay, now tell me about the business angle. Is it true that you've poached some of her catering and event contracts?"

He hesitated, glancing from me to Luz and back again. "That's different." He shifted his weight. "*Poached* is too strong a word."

Luz harrumphed.

"You have to understand that Golden isn't a huge town." He held up his hands as if to surrender. "There are a limited number of catering contracts, so of course we compete for customers. But that's not personal, it's business."

Regina piped up as she studied her manicured nails. "Maybe some friendly corporate sabotage was *just business*, too."

"Not in a million years!" thundered Thomas, rounding on her. "But it was *personal* for you when she fired your slimeball of a husband, and everyone knows you're a conniving, unstable—"

"I just want to know where my cousin is!" Luz exploded.

Everyone fell silent.

Tears brimmed in Luz's eyes. "Don't you understand? None of this matters to me if Vicente's not okay. Everything I've done—every hard choice I've made, every compromise . . . it's been for my family. Vicente is my cousin. My blood. Practically my brother in some ways. I just want him back. Nothing else matters. Nothing!"

CHAPTER 8

*T*here was a long pause. Luz's words seemed to echo through the wine cave.

None of this matters to me if Vicente's not okay.

My heart went out to her. *We'll find him, Luz. Everything's going to be fine.*

Thomas reached for her hand, but she pulled away. He stepped back, a stormy expression on his face.

Finally, Regina broke the silence. "Well, that's another reason to suspect Thomas, isn't it? The fact that Vicente's missing?"

Luz's eyebrows knitted together.

"What do you mean?" I asked.

Regina took another sip of wine. "I mean, what do Bruce or I have against Vicente? He came to visit you on occasion, but that's it. We have no quarrel with him."

"You might object to the fact that he's here investigating your intimidation campaign against Luz," spat Thomas.

Regina stabbed a finger in his direction. "But it was no secret that Vicente didn't like *you*. He didn't like you even when you and Luz were dating. And she always valued his opinion—maybe even more than the opinion of her parents and brother, probably more than anyone's opinion except her grandmother's. Did you think you'd have a better shot with her if her protective cousin were out of the picture? Did you hurt him?"

Luz swayed on her feet.

I waddled to her side and guided her to a seat. "Take it easy," I murmured. "This day has been hard. But he's going to be fine."

"Thank you," she squeaked. She threaded her fingers together, her knuckles white.

Thomas shook with red-hot rage. "I. Did. No. Such. Thing," he hissed, stalking toward the door. "I'm going to find Bruce."

The door slammed behind him, and Luz and I stared at each other. There was a long, awkward pause.

Deliberately, I turned toward Regina. "Are you ready to answer some of my questions now?"

"Fine." She rolled her eyes.

Goodness. Did she have to be *so* unlikable? This woman was going to drive me insane. "Where were you and Bruce today between eleven and noon?"

"Wait." She sat up a little straighter. *"That's* when Vicente went missing?"

"Yes . . ." I said slowly. "Why?"

She paused, then let out a chuckle. "Well, I'll be darned. I guess that lovestruck idiot really didn't do it. You're gonna need to work on some other theories, Little Miss Detective."

I clenched my jaw.

A *ding* sounded from Regina's purse. She checked her phone while I scribbled a few more notes. The roaming moth fluttered toward me, and I waved it away.

"Would you like to unpack that statement a little?" I asked, exasperated. Was this woman incapable of answering even a basic question?

"Thomas didn't do it because we can supply his alibi. We were in town at the time," she said. "On behalf of his new employer, Bruce had an eleven o'clock meeting with Thomas at the Wine Jug—that's Thomas's business. Thomas is going to buy a thousand bottles of wine from him, for catering. They were meeting to negotiate the final details."

"So why did you go with him?" I asked through gritted teeth. "You don't work for a winery."

"Oh, I wasn't at the meeting," she said, "but I did drop Bruce off. Thomas was definitely there—I saw him through the window. Then I went down the street a couple blocks for a manicure." She held out one hand toward me and pressed the edge of her thumbnail. The neon-green paint smudged, almost imperceptibly. "See? The polish is still tacky. Oh! I have a receipt, too."

She opened her purse and gingerly plucked out a slip of paper, then proffered it to me. I took it. It was a receipt for $32 at Star Nail. *And it's dated today at 11:52 a.m.*

"After I checked out, I went back to the Wine Jug." She rested her chin in her hands. "Bruce and Thomas were just signing the papers. Then Bruce and I left, grabbed lunch at the café—it's called Darby's, between the Chocolate Shoppe and the theater. I don't have a receipt for that, but I'm sure the waitress will remember us. Then we went home."

"Where were you when you got Luz's call?" I asked.

"Home," she replied.

"You got here pretty quick . . ."

She glowered at me. "We live just down the road. We bought our home *specifically* to be close to Bruce's work." Then she turned her glare on Luz. "Now he commutes forty-five minutes. Not that you care."

I scribbled more notes.

After another *ding* from her phone, Regina said, "Well, this was a fun chat, but I've got to run. My friend Alice wants to grab coffee. She's picking me up from here. I'll just wait outside for her. She'll get such a kick out of my nail polish!" She stood and looped her purse over her shoulder.

"Wait!" I said. "One last question."

She sighed dramatically. "That alibi wasn't good enough, dear?"

"I believe your alibi," I said. "But if Thomas was at the Wine Jug when the power went out and Vicente vanished, you're right that I might need to find some new suspects. Did you or Bruce tell anyone about the circumstances around your firing? Another vineyard owner,

49

maybe? Anyone who might be Luz's competition, who might have seen it as an opportunity to run her out of business?"

She shrugged. "No, not at all. When he was interviewing for jobs, he said he was looking for a better work environment. We complained about it to a couple close friends, but no—no one in the wine industry. People might misunderstand why Bruce did what he did, you know."

I paused. "Of course." They'd kept it a secret out of a sense of self-preservation. They didn't want the story to get out any more than Luz did—which confirmed what Luz had told me earlier.

With that, Regina headed out the door, humming a Beach Boys song.

I let out a low whistle and looked at Luz. "You okay?"

She nodded slowly, sucking in a deep breath.

"Any thoughts on what just happened?" I asked. "Did anything about those interactions feel weird to you?"

She shook her head. "I know Regina came across as combative and shrill, but nothing about it surprised me. She's like that."

"Oh, I thought she seemed nice," I deadpanned. "Easy to get along with. Fun to talk to. We should all have a dinner party together."

That broke the tension. Luz snorted. "And no doubt Thomas seemed . . . controlling isn't the right word . . ."

"He seemed like he wasn't letting you say no, even though he was the one who blew up the relationship."

She tilted her head, her lips tightening in a look of annoyance. "That all seemed normal, too. It's just the way we've interacted for the last few months. I keep trying to friend-zone him. The alibis were solid, though, weren't they?"

"Assuming they all check out, then yes." I glanced down at my notepad and shuffled through a few pages. "It means that none of them cut the power today. They could have hired an accomplice, of course."

"Wouldn't that be great?" Luz muttered. "So, what do we do now? We didn't make any progress toward finding Vicente."

"Let's go upstairs and look for Bruce and your *abuela*," I replied. "Maybe Vicente's come home."

We headed out of the wine cave, and I groaned as I climbed the hill in the sweltering heat. I clutched my midsection. *You babies aren't making anything easy.*

But then my thoughts flashed to Jim and to my precious little Laurie, waiting for me at home. Despite everything going on here in Golden, I smiled. It wasn't easy, being pregnant with twins while building a career as a private investigator—but it was worth it.

Goodness, I'd only been gone half a day, and already I was homesick for my family! At least working as a PI gave me plenty of time at home—more than continuing in my old career as an office manager would have.

When we reached the top of the stairs, Luz's phone rang.

"Hello?" she answered. "Oh, Fred! Thanks so much for calling me back. Yes . . . nothing?" Disappointment laced her voice. "Yes, I invited Thomas here to see if he'd heard anything. Well, thank you so much for trying."

I followed her as she walked toward the front door. Through the big front windows, I caught sight of Fred's tow truck again.

Luz hung up and turned toward me with a sigh.

"Fred's back?" I asked.

"After we gave up our search on the golf cart, I texted him and asked if he could help us search as soon as he finished towing that car. He said the driver had called him back and canceled—someone had jumped the car for them, I guess—and he was able to start right away."

"But he didn't find him?" I asked, heart sinking.

"No. Not so far. He's still looking. He just ran into Thomas, though, and called to make sure I knew he was on the property."

"Why'd you call Fred in? Just curious."

With a half smile, she said, "I don't know. It felt right, I guess. Fred's the sort of person who's always willing to lend a helping hand. Driving a tow truck helps with that—he's always on the road, and often has a few minutes to spare. He always loves talking to people, too."

I leaned against the wall. "Do you like him?"

"Hmm? Romantically, you mean?"

"Yeah." One of the twins kicked my kidney, and I suppressed a gasp.

"I don't know," she said slowly. "Sometimes I think I do, but I haven't decided yet. He's only lived here about a year, and the whole town loves him—and his little girl! Julie is the sweetest. Such a smart kid, and as kind and helpful as her dad. She begged to come pick grapes when we were harvesting!"

"That's adorable." I grinned.

"We do most of our harvesting by machine, of course, but we have a specialty label that we make with hand-picked grapes, so I let her come out and help one day with that section of the vineyard."

"Why'd Fred move to Golden, of all places?" I asked.

"His sister lives here. I think he wanted a mother figure for Julie. Poor baby girl." Then she managed a little laugh. "Do you want to know something crazy?"

"Always."

"Fred once said something that almost sounded like he'd been a cop once . . . maybe even FBI or something. Then he backpedaled and said he'd misspoken. But I think he was just covering for a story he didn't want to tell. Or couldn't tell."

My brows knitted together. "If he used to be a cop, why's he a tow truck driver now?"

She shrugged. "Mysterious, isn't it? Part of me wonders if he might be here in some kind of undercover capacity," she said. "Maybe the tow truck thing is just a way to get to know everyone in town. Gather information for some kind of big operation. Maybe he's still a fed."

"Huh." I stared out the window at the truck. "Do you think that might have anything to do with the sabotage at the vineyard? Like, maybe he's investigating the same people who are attacking you?"

She thought about it for a moment, then shook her head. "No, I don't. The sabotage feels personal, somehow. And recent. I think Fred is a mystery for another day. Maybe even for another detective—we won't have you here in Golden for very long, after all. But I think there might be a mystery there to solve . . . someday."

Through the window, I spotted a silver sedan pull up next to Fred's truck. "Who's that?" I asked.

"Um . . ." Luz said, squinting. "That looks like Frannie Peterson's car." Then she gasped aloud. "Oh! Oh no! I have an appointment with her . . . four minutes ago! With everything that happened this morning, it completely slipped my mind."

"An appointment for what?"

Luz frantically rebraided her hair. "She's getting married next year, and we're supplying the wine . . . and she might even pick Castillo's as her venue. Oh, what do I do? With Vicente missing . . ." She looked at me, wide-eyed.

"Take a deep breath," I said. "How important is this meeting?"

"The Petersons are a big deal in Golden. It'd be huge for us to host the wedding and . . . if we're about to get some bad press because of the unlabeled wine, this could really help offset that, at least locally."

"Are you able to compartmentalize and focus on the meeting?"

"If I have to," she said, inhaling sharply. "You can't successfully run a business like this if you can't compartmentalize. There's always something major to worry about."

"Take the meeting, then," I replied. "There's only so much you as an individual can do in the search for Vicente. I think I might sit down with your *abuela* and ask her a few questions—see if she's seen or heard anything suspicious."

Luz's eyes widened. "I really don't want to worry her."

"Since she's not aware of anything that's been going on, I think I can phrase my questions in a way that won't draw too much suspicion."

She studied me, then nodded. "Okay."

"Frannie Peterson is here!" exclaimed a gleeful, elderly voice. A moment later, Gloria appeared from the hallway, a huge grin on her face. "Look, she just arrived! I saw her car pull up from the apartment window! Tell her to come around the back, and I'll serve you all food on the porch! You, too, Kate."

"*Abuela*, Frannie and I really need to have a meeting about her wed—"

Gloria waved her hands. "Nonsense, dear. You can meet on the porch, over tapas, just as well as in that stuffy wine cave. I never did see what your *abuelo* saw in that cave. My porch is much nicer."

"Where's Bruce?" I asked.

"Oh, he headed out to the vineyard to look for something, so he won't bother your meeting. He reset the air conditioning—it's working now, thank God" Gloria replied.

A slim, dark-haired woman climbed out of the silver sedan and rushed toward the door. Luz grimaced as the doorbell rang.

"Guess we're going to be having our meetings together, then," Luz murmured.

"It's okay," I replied under my breath. "I'm too pregnant to turn down more food. Besides, I'm a professional. I can handle it."

"I'm not sure anyone can handle *abuela*," Luz whispered, then threw open the door. "Frannie! It's so good to see you!"

Frannie looked to be in her mid-to-late twenties, and had one of those smiles that could light up a room. I liked her immediately.

"I'm so sorry I'm five minutes late!" she exclaimed. "I was talking with a customer at *The Nugget* and lost track of time."

"Don't worry at all," replied Luz, glancing up at the clock. "You're barely late, and I've had such a crazy day—to tell you the truth, the time got away from me, too."

"Well." Frannie grinned. "In that case, I'm glad both of us are discombobulated. *Abuela!* How are you doing?"

Gloria marched up to Frannie, her face alight, and pulled her into a hug. "This has been the best day, *Panchita!* So many wonderful people all in one place."

When Gloria released her, Frannie reached out to shake my hand. "Hi, I'm Frannie Peterson."

"Kate," I replied, my mind spinning. How to introduce myself? I opted for the cover story we'd given to Gloria—it was less humiliating than being trotted out as Vicente's fiancée. "I'm so sorry to intrude— I'm here with Luz's cousin, Vicente Domingo. I—"

"Where *is* Vicente?" interjected Gloria, clutching her chest. "He came all this way, and I've barely seen him. It's very unkind to his poor *abuela* to run off like that. I hope he's all right."

CHAPTER 9

*L*uz stiffened at her *abuela's* question.

"Vicente is taking care of something with his car now," I said smoothly, grabbing at the first safe excuse that came to mind. Then I glanced at Frannie. "We broke down on the drive up here. It was quite an ordeal."

"Oh, that's why Fred's here," said Frannie. "Will he be back at the house later? I'd love to say hi."

"He's . . . helping out with something," Luz interjected.

"Well, come on back." Gloria rested her hand on Frannie's arm. "You and Luz can have your meeting on the porch, and I'll whip up some tapas. Are you hungry?"

"I already ate, but I know better than to say no." Frannie patted Gloria's hand. "It's so good to see you, *abuela*."

Gloria must be the honorary grandmother of the whole town, I thought with a little smile.

"Well," said Gloria. "I'll just do a little fruit plate and a tortilla, then, *sí?*" The matriarch took the lead, still arm-in-arm with Frannie. Luz and I trailed behind. I snuck a quick look at my phone, hoping I'd missed a reply text from Vicente.

Still nothing.

"So," said Gloria. "Have you thought more about where you're going to hold the wedding? It would be perfect in the Grape Garden here. Oh! You'll be such a beautiful bride!"

"*Abuela!*" scolded Luz. "It's her wedding. We must let her make her own decisions."

But Frannie didn't sound bothered. "I'd love to get married here at Castillo's. Honestly, my biggest hang-up is just that I'm not sure if I want it to be a big to-do or not. I mean, it's my second marriage." She glanced back at me. "I eloped to Vegas when I was barely twenty—which was a terrible idea. The marriage was an absolute fiasco. But is it really in good taste to have a fancy wedding for a second marriage?"

"I think you can do whatever you want," I said. "It's your big day."

"And why not have a big wedding?" asked Gloria, patting her arm. "You didn't even have one the first time around. You deserve your day to be *la princesa.*"

We arrived at the kitchen, and Gloria waved us all toward the porch. "Go talk, and I will bring food."

I clasped my hands. "You've worked so hard cooking already. I'd love to help you make the tapas. I could slice the fruit."

But Gloria wouldn't hear of it. "No, no, no, dear. You are almost ready to have babies. You must sit down with Luz and sweet Franita."

Almost before I knew what was happening, I was ushered outside to the porch. For a moment, I stared at the sliding glass door. What had just happened? How had Gloria so expertly herded me out of the house? With a shrug, I took a seat on the closest wicker chair.

Luz smirked at me, one eyebrow half raised.

Well, you were right, I thought. *No one can handle Gloria.*

Though the weather was still hot, it felt pleasant in the shade, especially with the gentle breeze kicked up by the ceiling fan.

"I'm so sorry," said Frannie, smiling at me. "I think you were interrupted when you were introducing yourself earlier. It's Kate, right?"

"Yes!" I said. "I think I'd started to explain that I'm just visiting with Vicente. He brought me up here because—"

"They're getting married!" squealed Luz.

I stopped short, then forced a stiff smile.

"Oh, that's so exciting!" Frannie leaned forward. "He finally found someone to settle down with." She glanced at my baby bump. "And he's going to be a father! You must be something special, to have tamed that one. Are you going to have the wedding here at the vineyard?"

I didn't dare make eye contact with Luz. "Well," I said carefully. "It might be more accurate to say we *hope* to get married. There are a few things that aren't settled quite yet."

For a beat, there was an awkward silence.

Then Luz said, "Kate, do you remember the tow-truck driver who helped you out? Fred? Well, Frannie's brother is married to Fred's sister! Small-town coincidences, huh?"

Ah. No wonder Luz had opted to use Vicente's terrible cover story with Frannie. Fred and Frannie knew each other—were practically extended family. If we used competing stories, word would get around.

So, I set aside my feelings and offered them both a smile. "Oh, Fred was so helpful this morning. He seems very nice."

"Fred is great," said Frannie. "Did he show you a picture of his daughter? Isn't she a cutie?"

"Yes! He had a picture on his dashboard."

Frannie's brow wrinkled. "Wait, if Fred picked you up *this morning,* why is he still here?"

The sliding glass door opened, and Gloria emerged with a tray—a fruit and cheese platter, plus two glasses of red wine and three glasses of ice water.

Frannie continued, "I saw him out by one of the outbuildings, with Thomas Lovelien, of all people. Looked like they were searching for something."

Gloria set the tray down on the porch's coffee table and pulled up short. "You saw who, dear?"

"Fred," Frannie replied.

"Fred and Thomas were searching for something? Together?" Gloria asked, her eyes darting to Luz.

Luz looked startled.

Gloria murmured, "Bruce left right away after he reset the air conditioning, but his car is still here . . . he said he needed to look for something." She straightened and stared at her granddaughter. "What is going on? You are hiding something from me."

"Nothing," Luz said quickly. "Everything's fine."

"*Nieta*, I'm old, but I'm no *tonta*. What is wrong? Is Vicente really taking care of his car?" The wrinkles lining her forehead deepened. Her piercing eyes shifted to me, and I took a sip of water to hide from her gaze.

"Everything is fine, *abuela*." Luz deliberately reached out and grabbed a piece of cheese. "They're just working on a project to help me out."

"What kind of project?" Gloria crossed her arms over her chest.

Then a sizzling sound came from the kitchen. The old woman cast one last suspicious glance at Luz, then vanished back inside, sliding the door closed behind her.

Luz let out a relieved sigh. "That pan sizzling saved the day," she whispered. "I was running out of excuses. She knows something's up."

Frannie was sitting up, her head cocked. "I . . . said something wrong, didn't I? I'm so sorry. I—"

"No," Luz interjected. "You didn't know." She raked a hand through her hair. "I'm so sorry. Today has been a lot. I can't say more right now, but . . . there's a situation, and we're trying not to worry her."

Concern shone in Frannie's eyes. "Do we need to put off the meeting? I can come back another day."

Luz shook her head. "No, no. This is fine."

"All right, then," Frannie said, reaching for a cluster of grapes. "As soon as we eat those tortillas, would you mind giving me a tour of the winery? I've seen it all before, of course, but I want to look at everything with the wedding in mind. I'd either like to do a big, beautiful wedding here, or something small—just family and five or ten of our closest friends—in my parents' backyard. I think it'll be really helpful to visualize both."

"Of course," Luz replied. "I'd be delighted to. Good thing the rain hasn't started yet! Kate, do you want to stay here and keep *abuela* company?"

I considered the question. Luz was giving me an opportunity to chat with Gloria, but . . . it was too late for that. Now that Gloria's suspicions had been raised, I couldn't glean information from her without causing alarm. Besides, an idea was brewing in my mind. I wanted to do a little research—which I couldn't do here on the porch where my phone had zero bars.

"I think I'll come with you, if that's all right," I said.

Luz shrugged. "Sure. If that's what you think is best."

Frannie glanced from me to Luz, a quizzical expression on her face, but she didn't pry.

For a couple minutes, Luz and Frannie discussed the logistics of holding the wedding at Castillo's. Then the door slid open again, and Gloria came out with the tray, carrying a tortilla for each of us. The savory smell tickled my nostrils.

As we ate, Gloria sat on the wicker glider, watching us with a cautious expression. But, to my relief, she didn't ask more questions about Vicente's whereabouts. We finished, and Frannie stood.

"*Abuela*," she said, "we're off to tour the winery grounds now so that I can visualize what my wedding would look like here, but it was so wonderful to see you and to eat your excellent cooking."

Gloria beamed, though the grooves on her face still ran deeper than normal. "I'm so glad you are here, *Panchita*. I do hope you'll get married here. You will be such a beautiful bride. *Guapa!*"

Frannie reached out and squeezed Gloria's hand, and then we departed, walking down the stairs to the grass. As soon as we emerged from the shade, I regretted my decision to join them. The sun beat down on us like we'd been thrown in the oven of Hansel and Gretel's witch. I searched the sky for the promised rainclouds. For the most part, the sky was clear, but some dark cloud cover to the west looked promising.

I wouldn't mind a downpour, especially if it cooled things off.

What I wouldn't give to be back in windy, foggy San Francisco—where there were no cell phone dead zones!

"So," said Frannie, "I'm open to the Grape Garden idea, but I had another thought about where we might put a wedding tent—can we take a look at that grove of trees behind the old barn? Near the pond?"

"Of course!" replied Luz. "I know just the place. A tent would be lovely there."

I glanced down at my cell phone. One bar. Enough to send a text message, but not to make a phone call or do any research on the internet.

"Would you excuse me a moment?" I asked. "I need to make a call. Is there somewhere that usually gets better cell service?"

Luz waved back toward the house. "The area around the driveway is the best for most cell carriers."

"Thanks!" I peeled off from the group and headed toward the driveway. After about fifteen steps, my phone showed two bars. "That's better," I murmured.

I reached a gravel path that ran parallel to the driveway and walked along it. As I went, I opened up my browser and searched for information on Castillo's Vineyard and its wines. I found the awards it had won—including the local award from this year.

Could I figure out who had been shut out of the awards? If I needed more suspects, a rival vineyard owner seemed as good a choice as any.

Then again, maybe the power outage had been a fluke, and maybe Vicente was just out there chasing a lead.

But the sick feeling in my stomach told me that none of that was true. That something had gone terribly wrong. After solving ten cases over the last year, I'd learned to trust my instincts.

I pulled up a list of the other vineyards in the county. Maybe I could send the list to Galigani, and he could run the owners through his PI database, to see if there was anything suspicious in their backgrounds.

Before I finished compiling the list, my phone rang. Jim's name appeared on the screen.

"Hey," I answered.

"Hey, hon! How's it going?"

At the sound of his voice, another wave of homesickness twinged in my chest.

"It's . . . crazy over here," I replied. "But it's so good to hear from you. I miss you so much already! How's Laurie doing?"

"She'll tell you herself! Say hi to Mama."

Silence.

Jim chuckled. "Hey! Peanut. Say hi! It's Mama!"

Then a tiny voice said, "Mama!"

My heart melted as I walked further down the gravel path. "Little duck!" I cried. "I miss you so much!"

"Mama!" Laurie said again.

"See?" said Jim. "She's doing great. Whiskers, on the other hand, may have gotten trapped in our bedroom for several hours this morning while I took Laurie to the park."

"Oh no!" I thought mournfully of my orange tabby meowing pitifully at the bedroom door. Though Whiskers was still technically a kitten, she was almost full-grown now—in her teenage stage at almost a year. "Is she upset with you?"

"Well, I think *she's* over it, but she did pee on one of my work shirts, so I don't know if *I'm* over it."

I snorted. "I hope it was that hideous puce-and-orange monstrosity my mom bought you for your birthday a couple years ago."

"No luck—it was the blue-checkered one. But I kind of like the puce one. It's grown on me."

"Grown on you like E. coli grows on someone with food poisoning," I said with a chuckle.

He snorted. "Hey, it's not that bad!"

I rounded a bend, and the gravel path widened as it curved away from the driveway.

"A genuine tragedy that it's the blue-checkered shirt," I said. "That's one of my favorites on you. But I bet you can get the smell out—just rinse the shirt out well and run it through the wash."

"Hot or cold water?"

"Um . . . no idea. Google it."

"Fiiiiiiiine," he said, affecting a longsuffering sigh. "I guess even you don't know everything."

"Pretty close, though." I grinned. "That's why you married me, right?"

"That, and you're a pretty good kisser."

"Only a *pretty good* kisser?" I teased.

"The best kisser." He sounded mournful. "Can't wait until you're home."

Through a cluster of trees, I caught sight of another building. A sign was affixed to the front. I squinted.

Bodega.

Didn't that mean *store*, or something?

The sound of typing came through the phone. "Hey, on that cat pee thing. Do we have an enzyme cleaner?" he asked. "The internet says I should pre-treat the stain with an enzyme cleaner."

"Yeah, check under the sink. I've had to use it on the carpet before." Then I let out a sigh. "I know I said this, but I miss you two so much already. Is my mom still coming over this evening to watch Laurie so you can go to your business dinner?"

"As far as I know. Otherwise Whiskers will have to babysit."

I reached the front of the bodega and peered through the window. Based on the equipment inside—and the sheer quantity of wine bottles—this must be the facility where Castillo's bottled its wine.

I glanced down at my phone screen. Three bars. Even better.

"Well," I said, "thanks so much for calling. Cell service is spotty here—the vineyard's pretty rural—so I won't always get your calls, but I'm really glad we got to connect." I headed around the building.

"Me too, hon," Jim replied.

All at once, I rounded the corner and stopped short, blood draining from my face. "I've got to go," I said. "We'll talk later." I hung up the phone before he could reply.

Poking out from behind the bodega was a man's black shoe.

CHAPTER 10

"*V*icente!" I yelled, speed-waddling toward the shoe.

As I drew closer, the chilling scene came into focus. A man lay behind the bodega, crumpled in heap.

Don't be dead!

"Vicente!" I called again.

But it wasn't Vicente, I realized when I saw the man's plaid button-up. It was . . .

"Bruce?" Why was Luz's old manager behind the bodega?

He gave no reply.

My mind raced, and I knelt next to him, feeling for a pulse.

"Thank God," I breathed. He was alive—his breathing was shallow, but his heart was beating.

Blood matted his hair, and a shovel lay discarded nearby. Based on the injury, I could only assume he'd been struck over the head with the flat part of the shovel. My eyes darted around the scene, but I saw no other signs of life—nothing to indicate his assailant was still nearby. Quickly, I dialed 911.

"Come on, pick up," I muttered as the phone rang five, six, then seven times.

Finally, a tranquil voice sounded on the line. "Nine-one-one, what's your emergency?"

How did 911 operators sound so darned calm all the time? I'd called the police a lot of times over the last year, and it still surprised me.

"I'm behind the wine-bottling facility at Castillo's in Golden," I said. "There's a man here who was knocked unconscious with a shovel. He's alive. Breathing."

"All right." The voice was a little garbled—service had been better twenty feet away, on the gravel path—but I could make out most of what she was saying. "I've got police and an ambulance on the way. They'll . . . less than ten minutes." The operator asked me a few more questions and warned me not to move the victim.

I put the phone on speaker so I could shoot off a text message to Luz. *Bruce unconscious behind bodega. Cops on way. Looks like attack. Come right away.*

The 911 operator kept me on the phone, her voice fading in and out. I answered her questions to the best of my ability, but pushed myself to my feet so I could get a better look at the whole scene. Bruce was lying in soft dirt. The gravel path didn't show footprints, but based on the patterns in the soil, it looked like he'd walked up the same gravel path that I had . . . taken a few steps off the path into the dirt, rounded the corner, and then . . . fallen.

I scanned the ground. No footprints besides Bruce's and mine. Then my gaze landed on an odd pattern in the soil. It was smooth—too smooth and too precise, like it had been recently disturbed. The smoothed dirt cut a swath around the back of the building, and then back toward the gravel path.

Someone had taken time to cover their tracks . . . literally. Then they'd escaped up the gravel path, where they wouldn't leave prints. If I had to bet, I'd say they'd used the shovel to disturb the dirt.

Had they left any other clues? Dropped anything? I didn't dare walk far past Bruce for fear of contaminating the scene with my footprints. From my vantage point, I couldn't see anything else.

I glanced at the time on my phone. Only two minutes had passed. Bruce looked awfully pale. *Stay alive. Please.*

With this attack, the saboteur had escalated to assault. More than that, I realized, eyeing the shovel. This attack rose to the level of attempted murder. That meant things were getting serious. And that really, truly meant that Vicente was in danger.

Because whoever was threatening Luz was prepared to kill.

Think, Kate. What's the motive for knocking out Bruce? For potentially killing him?

Bruce must have seen something, I decided. Which meant the saboteur had been back here, planning some sort of strike.

Unless . . . what if Bruce were involved? Maybe he'd gotten in a fight with his accomplice . . . or maybe his co-conspirator was trying to clean up a loose end. But this didn't seem like a planned attack. If it had been premeditated, the assailant would have made sure he was really dead.

No, Bruce surprised someone. Which means he might know the identity of the saboteur.

Unless . . . what if Bruce had attacked Vicente, and Vicente had struck back in self-defense?

Vicente would have called 911. He wouldn't have left Bruce for dead.

Bile rose in my throat, and I swallowed it back. "What were you planning?" I whispered.

"What was that?" asked the 911 operator. "You cut out."

I realized I was still on speaker. "Nothing. Just thinking out loud."

"Kate!" yelled a female voice from down the gravel path. Relief flooded my chest. It was Luz.

"I'm going to hang up now," I said to the operator. "The owner of the vineyard just arrived, so I'm not alone at the scene anymore." Without waiting for a reply, I clicked *end call.*

"Luz!" I yelled. "Back here!"

First, there was the sound of crunching gravel, and then Luz and Frannie appeared down the path. I waved my arms at them.

They arrived at my side, breathless, and Luz clutched her chest in horror as she stared past me at Bruce's shoe. "Is he . . ."

"He's alive," I reassured her. "But the injury looks pretty bad. Blunt force trauma. He'll need to go to the hospital. The ambulance is on its way, and so are police."

"Fred will be here in a minute," said Frannie. "I called him as soon as we got your message."

"And you still don't know where Vicente is?" Luz asked, her voice pleading.

"We're going to have to report him missing now," I replied. "Now that this has escalated to a physical attack, the police will take it seriously."

"Absolutely," said Luz. "And I know the cell service is iffy around here—I keep telling myself that whenever I get close to panicking—but it's not like him to just vanish for hours with no word."

In the distance, I made out the first strain of a siren's wail. "They're almost here." I walked back toward Bruce, still lying pale in the dirt. "Hang in there," I murmured as I squatted next to him again, feeling for his pulse. It was still going strong.

More footsteps crunched in the gravel, and I looked up to see Fred and Thomas running toward us.

"Luz!" called Thomas. "Are you all right? Did anyone try to hurt you?" He reached her and tried to pull her into an embrace.

"I'm fine," she said, brushing him off. "But Bruce was attacked."

Fred marched past them and strode to my side, looking down at Bruce's limp form.

"My gosh," he said. "I saw him walking around, what, an hour ago?" He glanced back at Thomas. "Not far from here. Is that right, do you think? I found you guys arguing about an hour ago?"

"You were arguing?" asked Luz sharply. Her stare cut toward Thomas. "What about? Did you do this?"

Thomas stared back, hurt etched on his face. "Of course I didn't do it," he spat. "Why would you think that? Don't you know me at all?"

"I thought I did a year and change ago when you cheated on me!"

He crossed his arms. "Fine. You win. I'm a lowlife cheater, and I never deserved you. But do you really think I'd hurt someone?"

"I don't know what to think anymore," she retorted. "The world's gone crazy!"

He scowled. "Sure, I came out to look for him, and we had words. But then Fred found us, and I figured the best thing to do was help search for Vicente."

The tension in Luz's frame softened. "I'm sorry for accusing you. Today has been . . . frightening. And I'm afraid for Vicente."

I tried to push myself up, but my center of gravity threw me off, and I landed on all fours in the dirt next to Bruce's unconscious body. With a wry expression, I tried again. Fred caught me as I pitched forward a second time.

"There you go," he said, helping me to my feet. "I'm so sorry we can't find Vicente."

Right. I'm supposed to be Vicente's fiancée. I summoned all my theater training, and tears brimmed in my eyes. "We'll find him," I said in a quavery voice. "We have to."

"Do you think . . ." Fred trailed off.

"Do I think what?" I asked.

"Well." He squirmed. "I'm so sorry to bring this up, under the circumstances. In the tow truck this morning, you hinted at some . . . er . . . relationship difficulties with Vicente. Do you think he might be taking a day to . . . clear his head?"

I shook my head. The wailing sirens were loud now. "I think something's wrong," I replied. "So, Thomas was with you after you found him arguing with Bruce?" Too late, I realized I'd dropped the grieving-fiancée act.

Fred hesitated, glancing at each person in turn.

"Well?" I asked.

He stared at me candidly, as if weighing my words. "You and Vicente aren't really a couple, are you?"

Whoops. My mind grasped for something to say, but I came up blank.

He shifted from foot to foot. "What's really going on?"

CHAPTER 11

$\mathcal{M}$y cover was officially blown. Fred had figured out that Vicente had lied about our engagement.

How do I respond? I took a deep breath. Instead of answering the question, I asked, "So, Thomas was with you after you saw him arguing with Bruce?"

He tilted his head. Though the kindness never left his face, I could see in his eyes that he was starting to put pieces together. There was keen intelligence beneath his relaxed, friendly exterior. "For part of the time . . . I saw them close to here, but nearer to the main driveway. It was a screaming match."

Thomas scoffed. "Bruce was screaming, maybe."

Fred side-eyed Thomas, then looked back at me. "Asked them what the problem was, and they said something about Vicente being missing and Luz accusing both of them of trying to hurt the vineyard. I figured it wasn't any of my business . . . I was just here to look for Vicente, like Luz asked me to. So, I moved on. Maybe five minutes later, Thomas caught up with me, and asked if he could join me. Said he wasn't going to try to reason with Bruce anymore."

Thomas threw his hands in the air. "Now, wait just a minute! I didn't phrase it that way! That makes me sound guilty."

"How did you phrase it?" I countered.

He opened his mouth, then closed it again. After a long pause, he said, "I think I just said I was tired of trying to talk sense into Bruce. That doesn't mean I had anything to do with this. I never laid a hand on him!" Then he looked at Luz. "And I certainly didn't try to sabotage your business. Maybe . . . maybe Vicente attacked Bruce? Ever think of that?"

Luz gasped aloud. "He would never!"

The gravel crunched again. This time, two paramedics were wheeling a stretcher down the pathway.

Luz looked up at them in relief, though her jaw still twitched with anger. "I'm so glad you're here. Thank you for coming so quickly. Bruce is back there." She gestured with a careless wave of her hand.

"Absolutely," said the taller of the two men. They rolled the stretcher past her to the very edge of the gravel. They left the wheeled cart on the path and crossed the dirt to where I stood next to Bruce. "You called it in?"

"Yes, I found him."

"Anything you can tell us about his injury?" asked the paramedic as his partner squatted down to examine Bruce.

"Looks like he was hit over the head with that shovel," I said, gesturing toward the tool in the soil. "Sometime within the last hour. He's alive, with a good heartbeat, but his breathing isn't as strong as I'd like."

"Thanks," said the taller paramedic. "We'll take it from here."

They got Bruce loaded up on the stretcher and whisked him away. No sooner had they disappeared than a uniformed police officer took their place.

"I'm Officer Barney Stent," he said, flashing his badge and shooting Thomas a glare that could have curdled water. He was about thirty, with a freckled complexion and red hair poking out from under his sheriff's hat. "Someone wanna tell me what happened here?'

I stepped forward. "Could I speak with you privately?"

His eyebrows knitted together. "Of course. Let's step this way. Everyone else, stay here—I'm going to want to get a statement from each of you."

We moved toward the trees—out of earshot of the rest of the

group.

"I'm Kate Connolly," I said. "I'm a private investigator, looking into a sabotage case. Nice to meet you."

He whistled. "A PI, huh? And a sabotage case? You don't hear that every day in a town like Golden. We've only got one PI here. He mostly creeps around the motel snapping pictures of cheating spouses."

Quickly, I explained the story: the ongoing sabotage at the vineyard, how Vicente and I had arrived to investigate, the morning power outage, Vicente's disappearance, and the attack on Bruce.

He nodded a look of concern in his eyes. "So, you want to report Vicente missing, too, I assume?"

"Yes."

"Think it could be the victim's wife?" he asked, tapping his pen against his chin. "Or does she have an alibi?"

"Mmm." I turned the question over in my head. "I suppose it could be her—she had an alibi for the power outage, but she did leave the wine cave in time to attack Bruce. Said she was meeting a friend for coffee. What makes you think she might have hurt him?"

"Eh, gossip gets around this town," replied Officer Stent. "I don't know the victim or his wife personally, but I know who they are. We have mutual friends. Seems like they have a rocky marriage."

"The wife did once accuse Luz of having an affair with him."

Officer Stent. "Well, I'd say she has better taste in men than that, but she dated Thomas." When I looked at him curiously, he added, "He's dated my girlfriend, too...well, now my ex thanks to him. I'm sorry to say, this whole situation is a mess. I'm going to have to radio in for backup, or it'll look like a conflict of interest that I'm investigating my ex's ex. To be fair, he gets around. He's got a lot of exes in town."

I seized on the opportunity. "Do you know him well? I know this is an awkward question, but . . . off the record, do you think Thomas is capable of sabotaging Luz's business like this?"

He scuffed his feet in the dirt. "This is *very* off-the-record, and if you repeat it to anyone, I'll deny I said it, but you're a lot further on in this investigation than we are, so . . . the notes, the power outage, even the cyberattack? Yes, without a doubt, he's capable of doing crap like that. But . . . I have a hard time imagining him breaking into her house or hitting someone over the head with a shovel. He's an entitled jerk, and half the men and women in town hate him, but anything that involves physical violence? Not his MO, in my opinion."

"Thank you. I won't repeat a word. This is very helpful as I put the puzzle together."

He reached for her radio. "Gotta call this in now. We'll get a team of officers and our K-9 unit out here to search for Vicente. And I'll get someone else to interview that pain in the you-know-what." He jerked his thumb toward Thomas.

Fred walked toward us, waving his phone in the air. "Officer, I just got a call about a car that needs towing. Would you mind if I gave you my statement now?"

"Sure thing," he said, wiping sweat off his forehead. "Kate, thanks for your help. We'll talk soon. Everyone can go back to the winery— I'll tell backup to go there to take your statements. Too darn hot to make you guys stand around here." He nodded toward my baby bump. "Especially you."

I shuffled back to the group and told everyone we could go back to the air conditioning.

"Good," muttered Thomas, glancing sheepishly at Officer Stent. "Let's get out of here."

For Officer Stent's sake, I didn't let on that I knew Thomas had broken up yet another relationship. I just enjoyed the delicious irony. *Maybe you should think twice about leaving a trail of broken hearts all around town, sir.*

Luz, Frannie, Thomas, and I walked wordlessly up the gravel path. Sweat stains soaked my shirt, and I couldn't wait to change. Even my extra-strength antiperspirant couldn't stand up to this heat. I glanced down at the lavender blouse and realized in horror that the pit stains were clearly visible.

Oh no! Do I smell?

In an attempt to retain some shred of dignity, I scratched the back of my neck while angling my head down and taking a whiff.

Oh. No.

I smelled, all right. Like rancid blue cheese. No, that wasn't an adequate description. I smelled like a skunk had sprayed in a pigpen. Or . . . like a wet dog with onion breath.

I sniffed again.

Definitely a wet dog with onion breath.

It was time for a fresh shirt. As soon as I got back to the winery . . .

Oh. No. No. No. No.

My suitcase was still in the back of Vicente's car—which was at the mechanic shop! I eyed Luz's slim frame. She was probably two sizes smaller than I'd been *before* I got pregnant with Laurie—there was no way she had anything that would fit me now that I was eight months pregnant with twins.

Am I . . . going to be stuck in this shirt until tomorrow when the car is fixed?

I reminded myself to be reasonable—we could drive to the mechanic shop and pick up the suitcases as soon as Officer Anderson came to take our statements. Unless we were stuck at the winery until after the mechanic closed . . .

When *did* the mechanic close?

The path curved, and then the paved driveway came into view, running parallel to the gravel. We cut across the grass and headed up the driveway toward the house.

I studied the cars in the parking lot. Fred's tow truck was still here, as was Frannie's silver sedan. But there were three other cars, too. I searched my memory. There had been other cars here before—I'd caught a glimpse of them when Frannie arrived—but I didn't think there'd been so many.

"Luz, do you park your car in the lot?" I asked.

She shook her head. "*Abuela* and I both keep our cars in the garage around the corner. That's Frannie's Honda, Thomas's Kia, Bruce's truck, and . . . I don't recognize the Prius."

"The Prius is Alice McCleary's," said Frannie. "She's an English lit professor at the community college. But why's she here?"

"Alice? Isn't that the friend Bruce's wife was going to coffee with?" I asked. "Alice was going to pick her up."

Luz nodded grimly. "Looks like Regina never left."

CHAPTER 12

$\mathcal{W}$e walked into the air conditioning, and all four of us let out simultaneous sighs of relief. I glued my elbows to my sides to try to keep my odoriferous fragrance under wraps. Maybe I could sneak into Luz's bathroom and look for perfume to cover it up?

Then I imagined the scent of warm vanilla sugar mingled with wet dog and onion breath.

New plan. What if I wash the body odor out with soap and water and dry the shirt with her hair dryer?

I chided myself. *Focus on the case, Kate. Don't get distracted by your own vanity.*

"First things first—let's find Regina," I said. "We've had one disappearance and one assault already. We need to make sure she's all right." *If she's not the one behind it all . . .*

"Should we split up and search the buildings?" asked Luz, pulling her hair down from her braid.

"No, we should stay together," Thomas muttered. His gaze flicked around the room as if he expected an assailant to jump out from behind a potted plant. "Haven't you ever seen a horror movie? Splitting up is a good way to get murdered one by one."

Frannie rolled her eyes. "Don't be so dramatic. No one's getting murdered."

Thomas shrugged. "You're not the one being accused of hurting Bruce and Vicente," he retorted. "In any case, I want a clear alibi if anyone else takes a shovel to the head."

"He has a point," I said. "I do think it's better if we stay together for now. Let's check the wine cave."

We made our way to the back door and down the hill. The door to the wine cave was ajar, and I caught a glimpse of glowing lights within.

"Did we turn the lights off when we left?" I asked.

"I turned off the track lighting," said Luz, "but the string lights are always on. But . . . I definitely closed the door."

I took the lead, gripping the handle with white-knuckled fingers. Breath held, I pushed the door open.

Regina was sitting at one of the tables, a half-empty glass of white wine in front of her. "Oh, there you are!" she said halfheartedly. "I was beginning to hope I wouldn't have to see any of you for the rest of the day."

"I thought you'd gone for coffee with your friend," I replied.

"She wanted Bruce to join us." Regina drummed her neon-green fingernails on the table. "Idiot let his phone die, so we're waiting for him to come back from his hangout with Gloria. If he's not back soon, though, I think we're just going to leave without him. What is he doing—decorating sugar cookies at Grandma's house?" She snorted at her own joke.

"Where's Alice?" I asked.

"She wanted to take a walk around the lake while we waited, but I thought it was way too hot. I mean, I'm wearing jeans." She gestured at her outfit. "California in the summer is the worst. If Bruce weren't a grape expert, I'd move somewhere cooler. The Pacific Northwest, maybe, or Colorado. I guess we could move to the Columbia Gorge area . . ."

I tuned out her prattle. *Regina doesn't have an alibi for Bruce's attack.*

Luz sank onto a wine-barrel seat across the table from Regina. "I've got some bad news," she said carefully.

"Oh?" Regina looked bored.

"Bruce just went to the hospital by ambulance," said Luz.

Regina sat upright, paling. "What? Is he all right?"

I interjected, "He was alive, with good vitals. But he took a significant blow to the head and was knocked unconscious."

She stood up so fast she nearly knocked over her wine-barrel chair. "I . . . I have to go. I have to go to the hospital. I'm sorry. Tell Alice what happened. I'm so sorry. Sorry!"

She ran out the door, leaving us in tense silence. I tried to weigh what had just happened. Was Regina's reaction the panic of a loving wife? Or over-the-top acting to deflect suspicion?

"I feel so bad for her," said Frannie with a sigh. "What a shock."

"Mmm, I don't know." Thomas sat next to Luz. "I'm suspicious of her. She's infamously volatile."

"You can say that again," muttered Luz. She scooted away from Thomas, almost imperceptibly. "Although I wouldn't say I'm necessarily suspicious of her."

"She and Bruce have been explosive for years." Thomas rested his elbows on the tabletop. "Even if she's not the freak who sabotaged the winery, I bet she attacked Bruce. She heard about all the weird things happening and saw her chance to get away with murder and pin the blame on someone else."

Frannie shook her head. "She looked really shocked. Do you think she's that good an actress?" Then she wrinkled her nose. "What's that smell? Did something die down here?"

The blood drained from my face. *I'm that smell. And I'm pretty sure I just died of embarrassment.*

Luz and Thomas looked around, sniffing the rank air. In the enclosed space of the wine cave, it was starting to become overpowering. They grimaced in unison.

"What *is* that?" asked Thomas.

My first instinct was to deny it, to try to frame something else—anything else—for my body odor crime. We were basically in a basement—of course it would be musty. Maybe the wine Regina had been drinking had gone sour.

But there was no hiding the evidence—the scent trail would lead straight to me. I was caught red-handed. *Time to face the music.*

"It's me," I squeaked. "Guess my deodorant didn't stand up to all that heat. I'm going to blame being pregnant with twins. It's a pretty good catch-all excuse for everything, to be honest. Especially when I want to eat a lot of sugar, or something. I always blame the twins for that." I was rambling, but it was hard to stop. My face felt *so* warm. This was absolutely humiliating. Maybe even more humiliating than pretending to be Vicente's fiancée. "And I can't change my shirt because my suitcase is still in Vicente's car, which is in town, and—"

Frannie shrieked. "Oh! I'm so sorry! I didn't mean . . ."

Luz's hand flew to her mouth, her eyes wide with suppressed laughter.

Thomas chortled, not even trying to hide his amusement. "So, is that what it means when a detective says something *doesn't smell right?* Guess you've solved one case already, Miss Private Investigator."

"I knew it!" Frannie exclaimed. "I thought you were a PI! Are you really engaged to Vicente? Fred didn't think you were—I guess because of the way you were asking questions—but . . . was that just your PI training kicking in?"

Well, there goes the last trace of my cover story . . . But at least I had a chance to reclaim some of my self-respect. If my treacherous armpits hadn't poisoned the rest of my dignity.

"I'm happy to say I have never been romantically involved with Vicente Domingo," I said, managing a tight smile. "I'm married, actually. Vicente and I know each other professionally—we worked together on a few cases back in San Francisco, and he invited me to help him on a case here in Golden."

"And now he's missing?" gasped Frannie. "Because he was investigating something? What on earth were you guys looking into?"

I deferred to Luz.

With a long sigh, Luz rubbed her eyes. "Someone's been threatening the winery. For a few weeks. I asked Vicente to come look into it."

"Whoa," said Frannie. "That's crazy! But let me know if you want any help . . . I don't have as much experience as you, but my fiancé was accused of murder recently, and I solved that case. I'm sorry. It's probably stupid of me to offer."

76

"You solved a murder case?" I exclaimed. "That's incredible. I'm thrilled to meet another PI-in-the-making."

Frannie offered a shy smile. "I don't know that I'd go that far. I'm just an amateur, really."

"But you solved a murder case, which means you have good instincts."

Thomas chuckled. "Bet she could have solved the Case of the Armpit Stank if you hadn't confessed."

Heat flushed my face, and Luz shot Thomas a dirty look.

"Kate," she said, "would you like a clean shirt from the gift shop? It's the least I can do after all the work you're putting in. I'm so sorry we didn't think to get your suitcase here."

"Does the gift shop sell deodorant?" I asked hopefully.

At that, she laughed aloud. "No, but you're actually in luck. There was a buy-one-get-one sale on deodorant a couple weeks ago, so I have an unopened stick."

"You mean the rest of us are in luck," quipped Thomas.

"Let's head back to the house," said Luz, ignoring Thomas.

One blessed trip to the bathroom later, I finally felt clean—I'd managed a sponge bath, put on fresh deodorant, and squeezed my way into a men's XL T-shirt. It was the least-flattering shirt I'd ever worn—tight around my baby bump and as baggy as a potato sack everywhere else—but I tugged it down as far as I could with a sigh of relief. I'd take clownish proportions over pit stains any day.

I pushed open the bathroom door and shuffled into the living room where the three of them awaited me. "Thank you so much," I called to Luz. "I feel human again."

Thomas cocked his head. "What's that smell?"

Luz slugged him in the shoulder. "Would you stop that? It wasn't funny before, and it's still not funny. The woman is pregnant with twins!"

"It's just rude," chimed in Frannie.

"No, I'm serious," Thomas said, outright fear on his face. "I'm not making a joke. I think I smell . . ."

The acrid scent hit me, and I blanched.

"Smoke," I said.

CHAPTER 13

*W*e ran out the front door, scanning the sky.

"There!" Luz said in a choked voice, pointing out over the trees. "It's the vineyard!" Smoke was curling into the sky like a living thing.

I was already dialing 911.

For the second time that day, the excessively calm operator answered. "Nine-one-one, what's your emergency?" This time, her voice was crisp and clear. The cell service was better in this spot than it had been by the bodega.

"There's a fire. At Castillo's Vineyard."

"Yes, ma'am, we've already received calls about that. Fire trucks are en route to the location."

I hung up. "They'll be here soon," I said.

"What if Vicente is caught in it?" asked Luz in desperation.

I glanced west. The storm clouds had drawn closer. "Let's hope we get rain that slows it down," I said.

The door opened behind us, and Gloria shuffled out. "Luz!" she called. "I smell smoke. Do we need to call the fire depart—" Then she stopped, mouth agape as she stared at the sky. "Mercy."

Sirens wailed in the distance. I curled my fingers into fists. What if Vicente *was* out there somewhere? Officer Stent had said a K-9 unit was coming, but there hadn't been enough time for them to get here, much less to stage a search.

What if the fire department couldn't contain the blaze? We didn't currently have the wind that made California Octobers so dangerous, but we were in the middle of a drought and sadly, wildfires were springing into action every few days.

My throat tightened at the thought. If the rain missed us, or if it didn't slow the fire enough, the vineyard and winery could be wiped out. Heck, the *town* could be wiped out.

I flipped open my phone, checking for any new messages from Vicente. Nothing. Jim had sent a cute picture of Laurie, but even her chubby cheeks couldn't bring a smile to my face.

How had the day gone so terribly wrong?

"Quick," Luz said, seeming to snap out of her horror. "Thomas, help me haul hoses. We're going to wet down the buildings so that it's harder for flames to catch hold."

Thomas stuttered for a moment, wide-eyed. Finally, his Adam's apple bobbed, and he nodded.

Luz's face softened. "Thank you. I know it's a lot to ask because of ... last year. Kate and Frannie, take *abuela* to town where it's safe."

Gloria stood up straighter, her stern eyes fixed on Luz. "Do you think I'm going to run off to safety and leave behind my granddaughter? My legacy? The vineyard I've spent my whole life building?"

Frannie stepped forward and rested a hand on Gloria's arm. "*Abuela*, please ..."

But Gloria didn't drop her gaze.

After a moment, Luz yielded. "All right, then," she said. "Frannie and *abuela*, stay here and focus on wetting down the front of the house and the flower beds. But Frannie—keep an eye on the situation. If it looks like the fire is heading toward the road, like it might trap us here, get *abuela* in the car and drive as fast as you can away from here."

"I will," said Frannie, her chin set with determination.

Luz glanced at me. "Kate, stay with them."

I opened my mouth to protest, but she held up a hand.

"Don't argue. We don't have time. You're pregnant. You can't run as fast if something goes wrong. This is safest for everyone."

79

My hand rested on my baby bump, and I nodded wordlessly. I was a pro at speed-waddling, but running wasn't happening these days.

Luz grabbed Thomas's hand. "Let's go," she said.

They ran toward the barn, and I hoped against hope that she could trust him.

Frannie pointed toward the side of the winery. "There's the hose. I'll drag it out. Kate, can you crank it on?"

"Absolutely," I said.

"*Abuela.*" Frannie motioned toward the smoke. "Keep a sharp eye out for us. Let us know if the fire starts coming this way so we can get Kate and her babies to safety."

With a grim expression, Gloria nodded. "I can do that."

Frannie darted toward the hose, and I waddled after her as fast as I could. By the time I reached the spigot, she was already halfway to the front door, lugging the hose behind her.

"Ready!" she called.

With all my strength, I rotated the handle, turning the hose on full blast. The hose sputtered, then twitched. A moment later, Frannie whooped. I headed back toward the front of the house, heart pounding. Frannie was spraying water across the stoop. As I walked toward Gloria, Frannie backed up, sending the plume of water over the siding and onto the roof.

It's working.

I glanced in the direction of the barn, but trees blocked my view. I hoped Luz and Thomas were all right.

The fire trucks screeched onto the road, then peeled into the vineyard, heading toward the flames.

The smoke was getting thicker, and I coughed. My phone buzzed once. Just a text message.

What if it's important?

For a breath, I ignored it. *Focus on the fire, Kate. What can we do about the fire?*

But something buzzed in my chest, warning me not to ignore the text. I pulled my phone out and looked at the screen.

Vicente Domingo.

I gasped aloud, then glanced at Gloria. She was staring out at the smoke, and I was glad she hadn't heard me react. With shaking hands, I opened the text.

Fanny Buddha.

My forehead wrinkled. *Fanny Buddha? What on earth could he mean?* Was Vicente trapped somewhere? Was he trying to explain where he was? I racked my brain. *Fanny Buddha.* If he was having trouble typing, maybe this was autocorrect . . . or talk-to-text.

Could he mean *Frannie*? But that didn't make any sense.

Buddha . . . I studied the keyboard on my screen. That could mean *bodega*, maybe? But what was *fanny*? I didn't know enough about the vineyard to interpret what that could mean. *Luz might be able to figure it out.* I glanced desperately in the direction of the barn. If Vicente was being held hostage somewhere near the bodega, there might not be time to go to the barn, figure it out with Luz, and then run to the bodega area and save him.

Who knew how quickly the fire might spread?

But someone else knows the vineyard every bit as well as Luz, I realized. My eyes drifted to Gloria. It was just as she'd said—she'd dedicated her life to this place. It was her legacy. If anyone could interpret this cryptic, mangled text, it was Gloria.

Immediately, I second-guessed myself. *What if the fright gives her a heart attack? What if I kill her by asking her this question?*

But as I looked at Gloria, at the steely glint in her eyes, at her ramrod posture as she watched the fire, I realized she was far less fragile than her grandchildren thought she was. She wasn't the sort of person to melt into a puddle at the first sign of danger.

She'll know how to save her grandson.

I marched toward her. "Gloria!" I called.

She snapped toward me. "Yes, dear?" Her posture was motherly, but beneath the softness, I could still see that taut strength.

"No time to explain everything," I said, "but I promise we'll answer all your questions later. I think Vicente may be trapped somewhere on the property."

Her eyes widened in alarm. "In the fire?"

"He's okay right now," I replied. "He just sent me this text message." I showed her the screen.

She squinted at it, then fumbled for her shirt pocket. "I need my glasses."

"It says, *Fanny Buddha*." I explained.

She squinted harder at the screen. "Fanny Buddha?"

"Do you know how to text?" I asked.

"Of course I know how to text. I'm old, but I'm not *that* old."

"You know how autocorrect sometimes changes words that you've typed?"

She nodded seriously. "Once, I was at the store and meant to text Luz to ask if she wanted me to get Pringles, except the text I sent asked if she wanted me to get pregnant."

Despite the urgency of the situation, I snorted. "Okay, so I think this is autocorrect, and maybe *Buddha* means *bodega*?"

Realization dawned on her face. "Of course," she said. "And *fanny* must mean *fan*. Fan bodega . . . *fanny bodega* . . . *fan in bodega*! That's it!"

"What does that mean? Where is he?" I asked excitedly.

"The vineyard frost fans . . . you know, those tall fans we use to keep the grapes warm during freezes?"

"I think I know what you're talking about," I said.

"There's a broken one that we've meant to fix for years," she said. "But we haven't gotten around to it. We've kept it in a back corner of the old bodega—it's the only building on the property with a tall enough ceiling for it. He must be trapped inside the fan."

"Trapped inside?" I blinked a few times. "How?"

"The fans are big enough for a person to climb up inside," she explained. "But it's a tight fit. Once, when a worker came out to repair a fan, my husband had to pull him out or he'd have been trapped. *Vamos!* We have to hurry," she said. "Fire can change direction fast."

"Frannie and I will go," I said, handing her my phone. "Call 911 and let the dispatcher know what's going on, so they know to send a firefighter to help. Then, can you keep spraying water on the building and flower beds?"

She gave a resolute nod and started dialing.

"Frannie!" I yelled.

Frannie turned toward me.

"Drop the hose and come with me! I'll explain on the way."

With a terse nod, she complied.

"This way!" I said, whirling around and waddling at top speed down the driveway.

Frannie caught up with me after about fifteen steps. "What is it?" she asked, breathless.

"Vicente sent a text," I responded. "It was garbled. Autocorrect. But Gloria and I think he may be trapped inside a fan in the bodega."

"The bodega?" she said. "Like, where Bruce was hit over the head with a shovel?"

"Yes." My words were coming in short gasps now. "We've got to . . . get him out before . . . the fire . . . reaches the . . . bodega."

CHAPTER 14

$\mathcal{T}$he smoke was thick and choking when Frannie and I
arrived at the bodega.

What would we do if the door were locked? There wouldn't be
time to find Luz and get a key. We'd have to bust down the door, or
break a window, or something.

Is it my imagination, or is it getting even hotter? Swallowing back the
bile in my throat, I pulled the front of my shirt over my nose to try to
block out the worst of the smoke. With my other hand, I reached for
the doorknob. To my relief, it turned easily, and we strode into the
bodega.

"Vicente?" I called, flicking on a light. I scanned the room. Machinery, I assumed for bottling wine. Empty barrels. Glass bottles. Then I
spotted it. A tall fan, extending up past the naked joists. "There—in
the corner!"

Frannie and I threaded a path amid the crowded room. As we got
closer to the fan, I called out again, "Vicente!"

"Kate!" Vicente's voice sounded distant. A faint banging noise
came from the fan.

I reached the fan and tapped on the side.

"Kate!" he said again. I squatted down, nearly tipping forward, and
peered upward into the shaft of the fan. Two shoes were kicking at

the sides. I was vaguely reminded of a beetle stuck on its back, legs scrambling for purchase against the empty air.

"How on earth did you get stuck in there?" I asked.

"Following a clue. Would you just get me out?" he sputtered.

He had a point. The smoke didn't taste quite as thick in here, but there was no telling how much time we had.

A chittering sound came from the top of the fan.

Vicente snarled upward. "Would you get out of here, you stupid rat?"

"You okay?" I asked him. It was kind of warm in here . . . was the heat getting to him?

A squirrel popped its head out from the top of the fan shaft, squeaking plaintively at us. Then it disappeared back into the tube.

I snorted. "I see you had company while you were stuck in there."

"Shut up," he muttered.

Frannie stepped forward and peered up the shaft, her forehead wrinkling. "Let's each grab one of his feet and pull."

"Sounds good." I tipped forward onto my hands and knees, letting my off-balance center of gravity pull me to the ground, then reached up and wrapped my hands around Vicente's shin. Frannie did the same. "On three. One . . . two . . ."

"Three!" We cried in unison, tugging at his legs.

He didn't budge.

"Try again," called Frannie. "On three. One . . . two . . . three!"

We pulled again, without any better luck. Vicente growled.

"How did you get yourself wedged so tightly?" I asked in exasperation.

He didn't answer.

Frannie scooted back. "This isn't working," she murmured. She burst into a coughing fit. I patted her back until she recovered herself.

"You good?" I asked.

"Does it seem like the smoke is getting thicker?" she replied.

Something squeaked from within the tube. I wasn't sure whether it was Vicente or the squirrel.

"Hard to say," I said calmly, hoping my words would soothe

Vicente. But Frannie was right—it was getting undeniably smokier in the bodega. We had to extricate him quickly.

I snapped my fingers. "We've got to find something that will act as a lubricant and help him slide out of the tube. An oil or a gel, preferably. Or a liquid, if we can't find either of those."

"I'll look around." Frannie shot to her feet.

"No oil!" cried Vicente. "If we run into any fire, I'll go up in flames like a dry Christmas tree on the Fourth of July!"

"Good point," I said. "Gel or liquid it is."

"Where are we going to find gel in here?" Frannie asked, opening a cabinet and shuffling through its contents. "Here's motor oil."

"No oil!" yelled Vicente.

"We're not going to use oil," I said, patting his calf.

"Got it!" cried Frannie. I heard two crashes and craned to look at her.

Shattering glass?

She marched toward us, a wine bottle in each hand—the tops broken off. She set the wine down at the base of the fan. "Found a case of wine that got left behind. Let's lug that ladder over," she said, pointing to the far corner of the room.

She helped me up, and we weaved through the machinery and grabbed the ladder.

"Steady . . ." I said as we hoisted it up. We held it above our heads as we navigated back to the fan.

Bang, bang, bang. Vicente's legs flailed against the tube.

Frannie and I set up the ladder, and Frannie climbed up several steps. "First bottle, please."

I handed her a bottle. She grasped it for a moment, looked down the hole in the top of the fan shaft, and poured the purple-red liquid over Vicente.

"Gah!" yelled Vicente. "Are you trying to waterboard me or something?"

"Would you rather be roasted?" Frannie demanded.

He had no response to that.

She poured out the last drop of wine and held the bottle down to me. "Next."

I traded bottles with her, and she poured the second one out over Vicente, swirling it to make sure the whole tube was coated in wine.

"You know alcohol is flammable, too!" yelled Vicente.

True, but . . . "Not as flammable as motor oil," I pointed out.

He grunted and kicked the tube.

Through the window, I caught sight of orange-tinted light. *We have to hurry.* Frannie climbed down the ladder, and we knelt at the bottom of the tube.

"On three," I said. She nodded.

This time, we counted in unison. "One . . . two . . . three!"

We pulled Vicente's legs, and his body abruptly scooched a few inches down the tube.

"Ow!" he yelled.

"Progress," panted Frannie. She glanced toward the window. The orange glow was unmistakable now.

It's coming this way. We're running out of time.

"Again!" I cried. I wouldn't leave Vicente behind.

"One . . . two . . . three!"

We tugged with all our might. He scooted down a few more inches. The room was hazy with smoke. I suppressed the urge to cough.

"Keep pulling!" Frannie said. "Don't stop!"

The door creaked open. "Is someone in here?" called a familiar voice.

"Luz!" I yelled. "We found Vicente!"

She gasped aloud. Thudding footsteps ran toward us, and she swept in at my side. "Chente!" she cried.

I squirmed backward—as a matter of simple physics, Luz would have a better center of gravity than I did at eight months pregnant.

"Help me pull him out," said Frannie.

Luz grabbed his leg, then flinched back, a look of disgust on her face. "His leg is wet. Vicente . . . did you pee on yourself?"

"No!" he practically screamed. "But I'm about to if you don't get me out of here."

"We couldn't budge him," Frannie explained. "So we poured wine into the tube to help us get him free."

Luz nodded slowly, her mouth quirked in confusion.

"Hurry!" I called.

They grabbed Vicente's calves. After two more tugs, he came flying out the tube, thudding onto the ground. The squirrel tumbled after him, bounced off his head, and scrambled up onto a piece of machinery. It chittered angrily in Vicente's direction.

"Stupid rat!" Vicente hissed back at it. "I don't like you, either!"

I stifled a laugh. Charming, dignified Vicente looked like a drowned cat. His hair hung in wine-soaked clumps, and two buttons had torn free of his shirt. The other buttons were red-stained. *Oh, and our suitcases are . . . still at the mechanic's shop!*

Poor man. He wouldn't even be able to change once we got out of here.

Luz grabbed his shoulder. "Let's go," she said. "I wetted down the building, but the fire's coming this way. Fast."

She helped Vicente up. He swayed on his feet, his hand flying to his head.

"Are you hurt?" Luz asked.

"I'm fine," he muttered. "Thank you very much. Just a little dizzy after being stuck in that dratted tube with that stupid rat for hours and hours."

All at once, plumes of choking black smoke streamed into the building.

"Roof's on fire! Let's go!" Frannie yelled.

We ran for the door.

Behind me, I heard a panicked chittering, and something about it pierced my heart. I halted and turned to look at the squirrel. Its tail was puffed out like a frightened cat.

"Hey," I said soothingly, inching toward it. "Come on out. I'll carry you somewhere safer, okay?"

I reached for it, but it leaped to the next machine, trembling. It squeaked at me and ran back to the tube.

"Fine, stay here," I muttered. But the squirrel turned back and stared at me. Like it was trying to tell me something.

"Oh . . ." I breathed, the answer hitting me all at once. "Do you . . . do you have babies in there?" My mama's heart broke.

The squirrel chattered rapidly.

I glanced back at the door. The others were long gone, running back to safety. But I remembered that there had been a stack of buckets in the corner where we'd found the ladder. I darted through the lines of machinery, choking on smoke, until I found the buckets. I grabbed the topmost one, and made my way back to the fan. The squirrel practically screamed at me as I climbed the ladder.

When I reached the top and peered down into the shaft, I didn't see anything. I looked at the squirrel. It leaped onto the ladder, scrabbling upward, into the fan apparatus above the shaft. I looked up.

"Oh, there they are!" I exclaimed.

I climbed two steps higher. Sure enough—there, perched on an old fan blade, was a squirrel nest, and inside were four perfect, tiny squirrels. I balanced the bucket on the rim of the shaft and carefully dislodged the nest, taking care not to break it. Heart pounding, I set the nest inside—it fit perfectly in the bottom of the bucket. I tapped the bucket and looked at the mama squirrel. "Get in!"

She leaped into the bucket, and I scrambled down the ladder just as the far corner of the roof collapsed.

Heat roared over me, and I ran for the door, sputtering and coughing. The squirrel let out a shrill scream. I pushed out into the open air, and my heart stopped.

The crackling flames leaped from tree to tree around me like I'd stepped into the pages of Dante's *Inferno*.

What had I done?

CHAPTER 15

J ran for it, desperate to stay ahead of the flames, bolting down the gravel path at a speed I hadn't known I could attain this heavily pregnant.

Then, ahead of me, I saw the fire truck, its flaring red lights almost lost amid the eerie orange flames.

Just get to the truck, I told myself.

A stray spark hit my arm, and I yelped and nearly dropped the bucket. *Almost there . . .*

A firefighter jumped off the truck and ran toward me. I met him halfway to the truck, and he reached to take the bucket. I gladly handed off my burden and continued my mad dash, the firefighter jogging at my side. The heat receded, and when I reached the truck, I turned around, breath heaving. Gray dots flickered around the edges of my vision.

The firefighter pulled off his mask and offered me some oxygen. "You all right, ma'am?"

I took a few long breaths of pure, sweet air. "Yes," I said in a trembling voice. "Just barely."

He glanced down at the bucket and laughed aloud. "A . . . squirrel? You almost got caught in a wildfire to save a squirrel?"

Jim will read me the riot act when he finds out. But I just stared at the firefighter defiantly.

"Squirrel *babies*," I said. "The mama squirrel asked me to help, and . . ." I rested a hand on my baby bump. "From one mom to another, I couldn't leave them to roast."

He gave the bucket back to me, his lips twitching in amusement. "You all right to go the rest of the way to the main house? You're not going to stop to save a family of possums this time?"

I managed a wry chuckle.

He continued, "Your friends are probably there already. We have the fire surrounded, but we're going to have you guys evacuate to town to be safe."

"Yes," I said, gripping the bucket handle in both hands. "I have it. Thanks for coming out."

He tipped his hat. "Just doing my job, ma'am."

I stumbled off toward the house, my feet scuffing against the gravel.

Oof. My free hand drifted to my head. I felt vaguely dizzy. The mama squirrel chittered at me and leaped up onto the rim.

"You're welcome," I replied, studying her puffed-out tail. "How about a ride into town to find a wildlife rehabilitator? Would that be okay? I don't like the idea of leaving you and the little ones here when we evacuate."

She chattered something that sounded like agreement, then leaped down to the nest to see to her babies.

"That's right—I did not go to all that trouble to save you just to leave you this close to the fire."

Though I knew she couldn't understand English, of course, I felt sure she knew that I wanted to keep her safe.

My lungs burned, and a coughing fit racked my body. I set down the bucket and focused on staying upright as my lungs tried to expel the smoke. When I caught my breath again, I snatched up the bucket and pressed on.

Yes, definitely dizzy. Grim determination drove me forward. The path curved, and the driveway came into view. The sky was white . . .

or dark gray. At first, I thought it was just smoke, but the color and texture were wrong.

Storm clouds! Hope flared in my chest. Were we finally about to get that long-promised rain? Oh, how I dearly, dearly hoped so.

I cut across the strip of grass and onto the asphalt. *There's the house.*

A small crowd was milling around the cars—Luz, Gloria, Thomas, Frannie, and Vicente. I waved at them, and Luz cried out in relief. Gloria crossed herself, and Vicente slumped against the car.

Now that the worst of the danger had passed, I couldn't help but chuckle at Vicente's bedraggled appearance. Before, he'd looked like a wine-drowned cat. Now, his skin was darkened with soot, and a fine layer of ash had settled on his hair, which stuck out in every direction.

"What happened?" called Luz, running toward me. "We made it here . . . realized you weren't with us . . ." Her words came in breathless gasps. "Told the firefighter who was . . . trying to evacuate us. They went looking for you."

"I talked to a firefighter," I managed. "They know I made it out."

"Did you get trapped?" she asked. "You were right behind us!"

We reached each other, and I held out the bucket, a sheepish expression on my face. "She had babies. She asked for help."

Luz stared at the squirrel, then me, then the squirrel. She burst out in hysterical cackles. "You . . . you mean you . . . we thought you were dead, and you were saving that stupid squirrel that had been tormenting Vicente all day?"

I slugged her arm and marched onward. "Hey, everyone made it out—that's what matters, right?"

A dark shadow crossed her face, and I internally kicked myself. Of course, the most important thing was that everyone had made it out—but that didn't mean the fire wasn't a huge deal for the vineyard. Luz had lost the bottling plant, plus who knew how many acres of grapes. And that was *if* the fire department really had the blaze contained.

And *if* we could catch the saboteur before they did any more damage.

We'd escaped the flames, but danger still lurked around us at every turn.

"Well," I quipped. "At least I proved you wrong. Turns out I can run *very* fast when I have to."

She snorted and shook her head.

We reached the others, and I pulled my phone out of my pocket and snapped a picture of Vicente.

When the camera clicked, his eyes bulged. "What did you just do?" he demanded.

I grinned. "Why don't you try starting out with *thanks for everything*? Or, *I'm really glad you pulled me out of there in the nick of time*? It'd be more polite."

He crossed his arms, entirely unassuaged. "Why did you take a picture, Kate?"

I flashed him a wicked smile. "For the joy of it. Plus, nothing you could ever do would give me better blackmail than this photo."

"Let me see it," he growled, lunging for my phone.

But I just tucked the device in my back pocket. "Sure thing," I said. "I'll text it to you."

He muttered profanities under his breath.

The squirrel leaped back onto the rim of the bucket and screeched at Vicente.

He stumbled back, startled, then glared at me. "What the . . . why . . . you . . . went back to rescue that infernal rat?" he sputtered.

"Why is everyone so shocked by this?" I muttered.

"That rat is the whole reason I was trapped." He threw out his arms. "It made a noise up there in that fan, and I thought someone was hiding or stuck. I went to investigate and . . . got wedged a lot more quickly than I expected."

"Did you think the saboteur was up there?" I asked, tilting my head. "Wouldn't it be dangerous to go poking in an enclosed space with a desperate person?"

"I—"

"Did you try calling out to see if someone was stuck and needed help."

He glowered. "I just acted, okay? I didn't really think it through."

I tsked.

"I had plenty of time in there to regret my life choices. Won't happen again," he muttered.

"That reminds me," I said, shifting the bucket of squirrels to my other hand. "How *did* you send me that text message? And why did it take you so long?"

"Oh, my text went through?" he asked, looking surprised. "That's how you found me?"

I nodded.

"Well." He shuffled his feet. "I tried to extricate myself at first, but I think I just wedged myself in even worse. My arms were pinned at my sides. My fingertips could just barely reach my phone in my pocket, but I couldn't pull it out or look at the screen or anything. I kept getting calls and trying to answer them, but I think I kept sending them to voicemail. Eventually, I took a little nap."

He fell silent, and I held up my hands, palms up, signaling him to continue.

He quirked his lips. "I woke up from my nap and smelled the smoke. Scrabbled for my phone again and had the idea to try to activate its voice command feature and send you a text. But I had no way of knowing if it had successfully sent, especially with the blasted cell service dead spots around here. Figured I'd have to get myself out if I wanted to live—was working on another plan when you arrived at the bodega."

"Like a knight on a white horse," I teased.

He rolled his eyes. "Don't let it go to your head, Prince Charming."

I scanned the parking lot. Bruce's truck was gone, but that was no surprise—Regina would have driven it to the hospital. The white Prius was gone, too. "Regina's friend must have made it back and gotten out of here. Does that mean we have everyone?"

"Yes." Luz tapped the roof of Frannie's sedan. "How are your lungs, Kate? Do you need to go to the hospital?"

I rested a hand on my chest and took a deep breath, then burst into another coughing fit. My airways felt a little tight, but not like I was struggling to breathe. It didn't feel urgent, but . . .

When I finally stopped coughing, I said, "If I weren't pregnant, I'd say no, but I might as well go, just to be on the safe side." *Plus, we can check on Bruce's condition at the hospital—and maybe ask his wife a few more questions.*

Luz nodded, concern written on her face.

With a chuckle, I added, "I've gone to the hospital a couple times already during this pregnancy, and I've definitely already met my insurance's out-of-pocket maximum—so it's no big deal to get checked out." Then I looked down at the squirrels. "Is there a wildlife rehabilitator we can take these little guys to? I know they still have their mother, but I don't know the first thing about where it's safe to put a squirrel nest. Plus, the smoke might have affected them."

Frannie stepped forward and accepted the bucket from me. "I'll take them to Maud. She's the town's wildlife expert and is always hand-raising some orphaned animal or another. She'll be able to assess them to see if they need any medical care and then figure out the best way to get them back into the forest."

Luz nodded brusquely. "*Abuela*, why don't you walk around to the garage? I'll go grab both sets of keys, and we'll all drive into town. Vicente, Kate—come with me. We'll all go to the hospital."

"I don't need a hospital," said Vicente. "I need a shower."

Lightning flashed in the sky, and a breath later, thunder boomed so loud I felt it in my bones. Then, all at once, sheets of rain poured from the sky—a genuine downpour.

The rain had finally come.

Frannie threw open her car door and set the bucket of squirrels on the floor, out of the torrent. "I'm going to take them in," she called, circling around to the driver's side. "I'll see you later."

"Rain!" cried Gloria, crossing herself again. "The Lord sent rain to save the winery!"

For a moment, Vicente scowled at the sky, but then the annoyance melted away. "I'm going to take a shower. This much rain means the fire isn't going to spread. Fire department will be able to put it out."

"*Sí.*" Gloria threw her arms out, tilting her face up to catch the downpour. Grinning, she wiped the water from her face and shuffled toward Vicente. "You must be starved. Take a shower, and I will make you something to eat. What would you like? Paella? You missed our tapas earlier."

He smoothed his bedraggled hair. "*Abuela*, paella sounds perfect."

As they walked toward the winery, Frannie's car pulled onto the driveway, and Thomas mumbled an excuse and walked to his own car.

"Well," said Luz. "Guess I'll take you to the hospital?"

"I appreciate it." I followed her into the house, where she grabbed her keys and a few towels. We mopped away the worst of the wetness and soot, and then headed down to the basement garage. I gingerly laid a pair of towels over the seat and climbed in Luz's small SUV.

"I smell like an ashtray," I said wryly as we pulled out onto the driveway.

"Better an ashtray than a barbeque," she quipped.

I chuckled. "Dark. Very dark." From the road, I caught sight of the fire. "Looks like it's actually in a pretty small area. That's a relief."

"Thank goodness," Luz murmured. "Kate . . . I'm terrified. Someone attacked Bruce—tried to kill him! And then they tried to burn down the winery. This has gone too far. Do you . . . do you think I should comply with their demands and close down Castillo's?"

"No!" I exclaimed. "We'll figure it out."

She gripped the steering wheel with white-knuckled fingers. "But what if we can't figure it out before someone gets killed?"

CHAPTER 16

*A*t the hospital, the nurse took my vitals, listened for the babies' heartbeats, and checked my blood oxygen levels with a device that attached to my finger. After a brusque nod, she wheeled in an oxygen tank and handed me the mouthpiece. "Breathe this in," she said.

I took long, slow breaths of the sharp, sweet oxygen. For the first time, it really hit me: *that was a close call.* With trembling hands, I sent Jim a text explaining the situation, just in case he saw anything about the vineyard fire on the news.

I didn't tell him that I'd run back in to save a nest of squirrels.

A few minutes later, the doctor came in, clipboard in hand. "Your oxygen looks good." She pushed her glasses up on her nose. "And there were definitely two strong heartbeats. Have you felt the babies moving in the last hour?"

"Yes," I replied. "I think one of them is using my kidney as a punching bag right now."

"Excellent." She made a notation on the chart. "Because of the pregnancy, we don't want to do a chest X-ray. There are a few other tests we could run, but because your symptoms aren't severe and your vitals all look good, I don't think those are necessary. You're free to go."

As she left, Jim texted me back. *What the heck, honey?? Are you sure you're okay???*

I'm fine, I replied with a little smile. *Mostly eager to solve the case.*

My phone pulsed again. *Are you sure it's safe?*

I promise I'll be careful, I typed. But nothing about my chosen career was ever fully safe, and Jim knew it.

Luz swept into the room, wheeling my suitcase behind her. "Ta-da!" she called. "I ran by the mechanic and got your suitcase. Vicente's, too. Thought you might not want to change back into your soot-stained clothes."

"Thank you! I might cry!" I'd never been so grateful to see a suitcase before. I climbed out of bed, double-checking the tie on my hospital gown.

"Meet me in the hall when you're ready." Luz grinned and stepped out, closing the door behind her.

I marched to the sink in the corner and dabbed the worst of the grime off myself with damp paper towels. Then I unzipped my suitcase and pulled out a pair of maternity jeans and a flowy empire-waist blouse. It was such a relief to put on truly clean clothes.

For good measure, I put on deodorant twice.

I left my dirty clothes on the chair and joined Luz in the hall, rolling my suitcase behind me.

"Hey," I said, "before we leave, can we check on Bruce? I want to make sure he's all right, and if he's awake, if he saw the person who attacked him."

"Yes!" Luz exclaimed. "I was hoping to."

After inquiring at the receptionist's desk, we made our way up to room 203. We entered the room tentatively. Bruce was lying on the hospital bed. He was still unconscious, but the steady beep of the heart monitor offered some reassurance. I scanned the vitals on the monitors. I wasn't a doctor, but I'd been in the emergency room often enough to read the numbers.

He's stable. We'd caught a lucky break. When he woke up, maybe he'd be able to tell us the identity of the attacker—and, by extension, the saboteur.

Regina sat in a chair at his side, clutching his hand.

"How is he?" Luz asked gently.

Regina snapped toward us. Venom flared in her eyes. "Why are you here?" she demanded. "Have you come to gloat?"

Luz held up her hands as if in surrender. "There was a fire at the winery, and Kate inhaled some smoke. We came to the hospital to make sure she was all right, and we wanted to see how Bruce was doing."

"Well, I don't want you here!" Regina leaped to her feet, knocking the chair onto the floor. "You know, I've had a chance to think about it, and I don't think you ever thought Bruce did any of those things at the winery." She jabbed a finger at Luz. "I bet *you've* been sabotaging yourself."

Luz sucked in a sharp breath. "Excuse me?"

"Think about it," Regina hissed, her gaze snapping to me. "The winery was in trouble. She was worried about her reputation if word got out about the grapes Bruce bought to save her sorry behind."

Luz balled her hands into fists. "Now, wait just a—"

Regina cut her off. "I bet she sent herself those notes. I bet she made up the break-in, and hired some Russian hacker to take down her system. Then she begged her cousin, the famed PI, to come investigate for her—so that it would look like she was desperate to find the culprit, when really she was just covering her own tracks."

"You must think poorly of Vicente's PI skills," I said dryly.

Regina cackled. "Oh, he's probably a decent investigator. I gather he's solved all kinds of cases down there in San Francisco. But he's biased. He's not even going to consider the idea that his beloved cousin, who's practically his sister, is behind it all."

"Why would I do that?" Luz demanded. Tears brimmed in her eyes. "Someone tried to burn down my winery—to destroy everything my grandparents built!"

"That was the plan all along, huh?" Regina bent over and set the chair back up on its feet. Then she sank down into it, staring daggers at Luz. "You wanted the insurance money, didn't you? You were tired of running the winery—or maybe you didn't think you were cut out for it. But you couldn't just sell it, because you were so terribly afraid of disappointing your insufferable *abuela*."

Luz's jaw dropped. "Don't you dare talk about *abuela* like—"

"So, you concocted a plan to make it look like the winery was stolen from you. Stolen by someone who was targeting you. And then you trotted out Thomas, Bruce, and me to take the blame. You didn't care how many lives you ruined!"

I held up a hand and stepped between the two women. "Now let's just take a deep breath here."

But Luz was trembling, her whole body quaking with anger. "I won't stand here and listen to another word of this." She spun on her heel and marched toward the door.

"You don't have to listen to me," said Regina, her voice cold and calculating.

Luz paused in the doorway but didn't turn around.

"But you'll listen to the papers when they run the story."

I stared at the woman, agape.

Luz whirled around and advanced on Regina. "Are you threatening me?"

"Oh, no," said Regina, her hand flying to her mouth in mock fear. "Are you going to knock me over the head with a shovel like you did to my poor husband?"

Luz stopped within inches of Regina. "I've never hit anyone in my life, but you're pushing me awfully close to the brink."

"Go ahead," spat Regina. "It won't change the fact that I'm going to take all of this public. From the very beginning."

"From the very beginning?" scoffed Luz. "You're going to tell the world how your husband went behind my back to counterfeit Castillo's famed wines? He'll never work in the industry again."

Regina just offered a malicious grin. "I think the newspapers will be interested to know that all of that was your idea—that you threatened to fire Bruce if he didn't buy those grapes, and that he quit because of a toxic work environment and because his conscience couldn't handle what you were making him do."

Luz squeaked. "I *fired* Bruce."

That stupid, smug smirk didn't budge from Regina's face. "Well, that's what *you* say. But that conversation happened in person. Even your precious *abuela* doesn't know you fired him. Your word against ours, honey."

Heat flared in my chest. I wanted to give Regina a piece of my mind—but one look at Luz, and I knew I had to keep a calm head. Rage emanated from her.

Time to intervene before this escalates. I rested a hand on her arm. "She's not worth it," I said softly. "Let's go."

Slowly, Luz backed away, though hot anger still pulsed from her.

As we moved to the door, I called, "Regina, think very carefully what you take to the press. It's your right to tell a reporter the truth, but if you lie, it's Luz's right to sue you for libel."

Regina's scoff followed us out the door.

Luz fumed as we walked down the corridor. "Why that conniving, no-good—"

"Deep breaths," I said.

She raked a hand through her frazzled hair. We turned down another hallway. Ahead, an *EXIT* sign flickered above a door.

"I didn't stage any of this," she said in a strangled voice.

"I know. She was just trying to get under your skin. I heard it from her own mouth earlier today—you fired Bruce because of how he solved the problem of the spoiled grapes."

"But what if she goes to the press?" Luz pushed the crash bar, and we strode into the waiting room of the emergency department.

"Then you'll tell the press the truth when they call you for comment. I'll back you up. Thomas will back you up."

Humid heat enveloped us as the automatic doors opened. We headed for Luz's car. The rain had stopped, but clouds still shrouded the sky.

"But even if we fight lies with truth, my reputation will always have a black mark." Her voice was listless. "The questions will follow me . . . this is so much worse than counterfeiting our wine. She's accusing me of crimes! Assault. Insurance fraud. Of trying to frame her husband. Of conning everyone I love."

"It's a sensational story," I said with a sigh, loading my suitcase into the trunk of the SUV. "That's what she's banking on. That you'll do anything to keep her from going to the press."

"The local news station would have a field day." We climbed into our seats, and Luz fiddled with the radio, landing on a jazz station. "And I know time will exonerate me, but it's so much easier for people to remember the first dramatic headline than the correction issued later."

"It will be okay," I said, trying to reassure her even though I knew it wouldn't do any good. "You have a great reputation, and that will help. People who know you won't jump to conclusions."

"I don't know."

We fell into uneasy silence as we pulled onto the road. Halfway to the winery, we passed a fire truck that was headed back toward town.

"That must be a good sign," I said, pointing to the vehicle. "They don't need all hands on deck anymore."

A ray of sunshine hit the car, and Luz managed a wan smile. "Guess the sun coming back out feels like a good sign, too."

I tugged my notepad out of my purse. "Can we discuss the case? I want to make sure I'm not missing anything."

She gripped the steering wheel harder. "Yes. I want to put a stop to this once and for all. It's gone too far."

"All three of our suspects had an alibi for the power outage this morning," I said. "And while it's possible that Regina or Thomas managed to set fire to the winery and knock Bruce over the head, I think we might need to expand our suspect pool. Can you think of anyone else who might have it in for you?"

She let out a long sigh. "I wish I could, but I really can't think of anyone. I mean, there are plenty of people who could have a motive in theory . . . other winery owners, or a crazy person who thinks we use too much water, or someone who wants to buy my land . . . but I really don't know of anyone else who might have a grudge against me. Certainly not enough of a grudge to start a fire in California in the summer. I mean, they could have gotten people killed! Burned down the whole town—or worse! Wildfires out here can get very serious very fast."

We pulled up to the house, and I groaned as I slid out of the car and grabbed my suitcase. I felt like walking Jell-O. Sunshine beat down on me with oppressive force, made more suffocating by the moisture evaporating off the concrete. I stared up at the sky. Though it was still mostly cloudy, the white canopy had parted above the winery.

"Why is it so darn hot?" I panted under my breath. "It rained and everything!"

Man, I loved San Francisco and its mild weather. How could I even *think* in this heat? How could I possibly solve a case when it felt like I was wandering in the Sahara Desert like a parched camel?

Luz and I walked into the winery, dragging the suitcases behind us.

What next? I thought through my options quickly. "I'd like to touch base with Vicente to discuss the case. He was out of the loop for most of today, so it'd be good to bounce ideas off him."

She snorted. "Well, I'm sure he's had a chance to shower and style his hair, at least. I bet he's with *abuela* in the kitchen."

I rolled my eyes as we set off down the hall.

"Knock, knock!" called Luz as we entered the kitchen.

Vicente and Gloria were sitting at the table, an army of empty plates in front of them. Sure enough, Vicente had showered and styled his hair—but in the absence of his suitcase, he was wearing a fuzzy magenta robe.

I stopped short, pursing my lips to keep from bursting into laughter.

"Hey!" Luz called. "Why are you wearing my robe? I'm going to have to wash that now!"

I snorted. "That's a good color on you, Vicente. You should branch out. Wear stuff that's not black. You could try lilac purple next. Let me get another photo."

"Don't you dare!" he scowled at me. Then he turned to Luz. "Wasn't my first choice, I promise," he said dryly. "But it wasn't like you or *abuela* had much that would fit me."

Luz rolled the suitcase up to him with a half smirk. "Well, here are clothes that will fit. Throw the robe in the wash on your way back. Run it on extra hot."

Fifteen minutes later, a fully dressed Vicente and I sat in the wine cave, staring down at my notepad.

"But it turned out all three of them had an alibi," I explained. "They were together in town at the time the lights went out and you disappeared. Plus, Regina had a receipt from the nail salon time-stamped for then. Except . . ." I scrunched my face. "Now it turns out your disappearance wasn't connected to the sabotage. What if the power outage was a coincidence, too?"

"Not likely," grunted Vicente. "Remember the note from this morning? *Lights out*, or something? And you said the main breaker had flipped, which Fred thought was odd."

"Right . . . so the saboteur was on the property at the time. Does that rule the three of them out as suspects?"

"Hmm . . ." He stood and began to pace the wine cave. "Not necessarily, if they have an accomplice. But let's think this through. First, Thomas."

I flipped a page, ready to scrawl out Vicente's thoughts.

"Thomas stands to profit from poaching business from Luz," he said, "and he might have also hoped to win her back. But I don't think he'd start a fire. Actually, I know he wouldn't."

"Too much risk of the fire getting out of control," I said. "Burning down the town?"

"That too." He nodded. "But, on a more personal level, Thomas lost his mom in a wildfire two or three years ago—a few months before he and Luz started dating."

My hand flew to my mouth. "Oh, how tragic."

"Yeah. I don't think there's any way he would have set that fire. Second, Bruce," he continued. "Maybe an accomplice attacked Bruce because their deal went bad?"

"Feels like a stretch to me." I tapped my pen on the countertop.

He waved his hand. "No, you're right. So, that leaves us with Regina."

My face puckered like I'd tasted something sour.

He chuckled. "Looks like she endeared herself to you."

"You could say that." I rolled my eyes. "She's very unpleasant. Underhanded, conniving. But, of course, that doesn't mean she's the saboteur. Necessarily."

"Sounds like you hope it's her." He studied me.

"I wouldn't go that far," I replied. "But she's horrid." I related the threats Regina had made at the hospital.

His eyes narrowed, and he swore under his breath. "Why, I oughta . . ."

"But," I said, "would Regina have started a fire? They live awfully close to the winery."

Vicente pinched the bridge of his nose. "You know, I don't think so. She's got a couple horses that she loves a lot. I don't think she'd have risked the fire spreading to her property."

"So, does that mean we're at a dead end? No leads?" I asked desperately.

Vicente replied with a grim nod.

"All right." I tried to think. "So, let's start at the beginning. See if we can figure out another—"

A shrill scream pierced my ears.

CHAPTER 17

*V*icente and I raced out of the wine cave and up the hill to the house.

My heart raced—had Bruce's attacker struck again? Was someone hurt?

"What's going on?" Vicente demanded.

On the porch, a police officer was handcuffing Luz, reading her Miranda rights. Gloria stood in the doorway, hand over her mouth. Two other officers milled around the front of the house—one I recognized as Officer Stent, the redheaded cop I'd met earlier that day.

"*Abuela*, are you all right?" Vicente ran to his grandmother, frantically scanning her for injuries.

"They're taking my baby!" Gloria wailed. "She didn't do anything!"

Luz locked eyes with me and mouthed, "Help."

I walked toward the officers, trying to look imposing. "Why are you arresting her?"

"Ma'am, I need you to stay back," warned the arresting officer.

"Officer Stent," I snapped. "Please explain this to me."

Officer Stent shrugged apologetically. "We got an anonymous tip that the fire was related to insurance fraud."

"Regina," spat Vicente. "She's lying to you."

"That's not enough to make an arrest on," I added. "You know that's very shaky ground.

Officer Stent glanced at the arresting officer, then said, "I'm sorry, but Bruce woke up and named Luz as his attacker."

"What?" I drew back. If that was true, it wasn't any surprise they were arresting her. "Did you interview him?"

"His wife called it in," he replied.

Ah. Regina strikes again.

Vicente threw out his hands. "And did his wife's voice sound a lot like the anonymous tipster's voice?"

Evidently, he'd reached the same conclusion I had.

"That's enough," said the arresting officer in a deep baritone. "You're welcome to call an attorney for her, but I'm not going to let you interrogate the police."

"Excuse me." I fished a business card out of my wallet and held it out to him. "I'm Kate Connolly, and I'm a private investigator looking into some suspicious activity around the vineyard."

He eyed my card but didn't take it. Something in the frown lines around his mouth reminded me of my longtime police nemesis, Patrick McNearny. "You licensed?" he barked.

I hesitated. Technically, I was still working under Galigani's supervision—and Galigani was a hundred miles away, *and* I hadn't talked to him much about this case.

"I'm licensed." Vicente stepped forward, offering a handshake.

The officer coldly ignored the gesture.

Vicente dropped his hand. "Kate's working toward her license under supervision," he said. It was a true statement—though perhaps it falsely implied I was Vicente's apprentice.

Well, better apprentice than fiancée, at least.

The officer pushed Luz toward the door. "Well, I'm sorry, but I can't work with a PI who's related to the suspect." He paused and gestured back to us. "But I will want to see both of you in the station later today. We'll want to ask you a few questions."

They left, but Officer Stent paused at the door for a second. "I'll take your card," he said to me.

I waddled forward a few steps and gave it to him wordlessly.

"Thanks," he said softly. "You don't think she did it for the insurance money?"

"I don't think she did it at all," I said. "But I don't think Thomas or the Stringers did it, either."

He raised an eyebrow. "You have a new suspect?"

I sucked in a breath. "Not . . . anything concrete yet. We're working on some theories." *Hopefully that sounded a lot more confident than I feel.*

With a nod, he said, "Well, keep us posted. We want to get to the truth, not just make an arrest and close the case." Then his voice dropped to a whisper. "Well . . . at least that's what I want. Detective McNamara back there . . . he's running for sheriff in the next election."

He let the unspoken implication hover between us. If the arresting officer were running for sheriff, making a big arrest like this could be a huge feather in his cap, a way to appeal to the voters.

But my mind stuttered on one particular detail.

"Wait. His name's McNamara?"

He frowned. "Yeah, why?"

I shook my head in amazement. Did McNearny have a doppelganger in every jurisdiction, lying in wait to try to stymie my PI work?

"No reason," I said. "Stay in touch, and we'll get this figured out."

The door closed behind her, and I turned around. Vicente's arms were wrapped around Gloria, and the two of them were speaking in low, lilting Spanish.

For her part, Gloria seemed to have calmed. She nodded brusquely at me. "It will work out. Luz is innocent. If we have to call Gary to come home. We will."

Vicente and I shared a look. Luz's brother Gary was the infamous "Gary the Grizzly" the top dog criminal defense attorney on the West Coast, who'd personally helped us both on more than one occasion.

"Don't worry, *abuela*, I have Gary on speed-dial," said Vicente.

Gloria was still looking at me. "You are not one of Vicente's clients. You came here to investigate with him. You are a PI. Vicente told me everything just now."

With a nod, I said, "I'm so sorry for lying to you. We came to investigate sabotage at the vineyard, and we didn't want to cause you stress—"

She held up her hand. "I'm not angry. You will solve the case, *querida*. You and Vicente. You will save Luz."

I swallowed hard. "Of course we will."

But how? We didn't have a single usable lead! And Officer Stent had all but implied that the ranking officer on the case wanted to make a high-profile arrest to further his political ambitions.

Gloria turned on her heel. "I made *polvorones de canele* earlier. It will help you think. Oh! When you go to talk to the officers, you can bring some. Maybe it will give them some common sense."

"Cinnamon cookies," Vicente explained. "They're very good."

Despite the dire situation, my stomach growled.

Vicente chuckled darkly. "Still hungry after a full day with my *abuela*?"

We followed Gloria toward the kitchen.

"She's a fabulous cook," I said. "But I'm eating for three, and I think those *pollos de canoli* are just the thing I need."

He burst into riotous laughter. "Well, a *chicken pastry* sounds terrible, but I expect you'll enjoy the *polvorones de canele*."

"Whoops," I said. "You knew what I meant." But I was too focused on the case to be embarrassed by the mispronunciation.

Silence fell over us. After a few more steps, I said, "She knows not to talk to the police, right? To not try to explain what really happened and try to clear her name?"

He nodded seriously. "She's Gary's sister. Of course she knows."

"I think we should call him and let him know what's going on," I whispered to Vicente once I was sure we were out of Gloria's hearing range.

But Vicente was already dialing. He and I stopped at the kitchen table, and I sniffed the air while Gloria bustled into the kitchen.

What a delicious smell!

"Gary, Luz needs your help," Vicente said into the phone. "She's been arrested for arson and attempted murder. Is there a lawyer out here you recommend? Can you make any calls?"

I could hear Gary's voice on the line but couldn't quite make out his words.

"Sounds great," said Vicente. "See you soon." He hung up and looked at me. "He's going to call a lawyer in Golden to get Luz out of jail. And he'll be here in two hours."

"Wait, who's going to be here in two hours?" I asked.

"Gary," said Vicente nonchalantly, as if the answer should be obvious. "The lawyer here will get Luz out right away, but Gary is coming."

Gloria let out a little shout of delight. "*Mi niño!*"

"Just like that? He's just dropping all his other clients and coming to Golden?"

Vicente stared at me. "This is his sister we're talking about. Besides, this should only take a few days to clear up. He can manage his paralegals from a distance and call in favors with other attorneys to make sure his clients are well taken care of. Now we just have to do our job."

I took a deep breath. *We just have to do our job.*

We couldn't focus on the stakes. We just had to buckle down and solve the case.

Easier said than done.

We sat at the table. I pulled out my notepad, and Gloria set a plate of delectable-looking cookies in front of us. I grabbed one and took a bite. The cinnamon-sweet goodness was every bit as delicious as it looked.

"Oh my gosh!" I exclaimed through a mouthful of cookie. "I need this recipe."

Gloria grinned at me. "I will write it for you. Normally I keep my secrets about food, but I will hold nothing back from you since you are helping Luz."

My phone rang, and I glanced down at the screen. Mom was videocalling.

She's babysitting Laurie, I realized. *What if something's wrong?* I held up a hand. "I have to take this. Just a second," I said. I answered the phone. "Hey!"

"Darling!" cried Mom. Her beaming face appeared on my screen, along with the very top of Laurie's angelic curls. She shifted the screen downward, so Laurie's cereal covered face was in view. "How is your trip?"

Jim apparently hadn't told her about the fire or my trip to the hospital—just as well. I didn't have time to explain *that* mess.

"Mama!" Laurie screeched, clapping her hands.

"Why, hello, my little duck!" I called, clapping to mimic her movement. "Mama misses you already!"

"As you can see, she's made a mess here with the cereal. She's a regular cereal killer."

Vicente raised an eyebrow at me.

"Mom," I said, "the case has reached a critical point, so I can't really talk right now—"

"That's your *mamá?*" called Gloria from the kitchen. "And your *bebé?*"

"Yeah," I replied. "Don't worry, I'm getting off the phone so I can focus on freeing Luz."

Gloria marched toward me and took the phone. "You focus on the case. I will give your mamá the recipe you wanted, and she can make it for you when you go home."

"Oh, it's really—"

But Gloria had already swiped the phone from me and was introducing herself to my mom.

Vicente gave me an apologetic look, but I shrugged.

"Mom lives for making new friends, especially if she can tell them all the dramatic details of her day." I tapped my pen against the notepad. "Okay, we need to find the saboteur, but the first order of business is clearing Luz."

"Yes," said Vicente. "Obviously."

"So, we don't have a viable suspect yet," I said.

"Unfortunately. Which means we need to figure out a new suspect list."

A light bulb turned on in my head. "Not necessarily."

He raised an eyebrow. "Explain."

"Well, we'll need a new suspect list eventually," I replied. "But it's like I said—our first order of business is proving Luz's innocence. We eliminate her like we'd eliminate any other suspect."

He snapped his fingers and stood up. "Of course." He paced the length of the table. "We prove she has an alibi."

"Exactly. We need to prove that Luz couldn't have knocked Bruce out or started the fire. Let's trace everyone's movements from the moment the power went out."

I made a list: *Luz, Gloria, Kate, Vicente, Thomas, Bruce, Regina, Frannie, Fred.*

Vicente nodded slowly. "We need witnesses who can attest to Luz's whereabouts and rule her out as a suspect."

Beneath the names, I sketched out a rough timeline. My eyes drifted to the plate of cookies. I reached for another one, and the cinnamon perfection practically exploded in my mouth.

Focus on the case, I chided myself.

"Okay," I said, staring at the notepad. "We need Frannie to go on the record that she was walking the property with Luz. That's the biggest time block that could potentially correspond to the fire. Most of the rest of the time, she was with me."

"Any other unaccounted-for time blocks?" asked Vicente.

I squinted at the timeline and added a scribble to one of the lines. "At this point, she went to check on your *abuela*, I think. But she wasn't gone long, and that was hours before the fire."

A look of relief crossed his face. "So, as long as she was with Frannie from the time you left them until the time you found Bruce . . . she has an alibi."

"And the arrest hinges on Regina's testimony that Bruce named Luz as his attacker." I clapped once. "If we prove she couldn't have hit Bruce over the head, they'll have no reason to take the anonymous tip about insurance fraud seriously."

"The case against her will fall apart." Vicente folded his hands together, squinting as if he were trying to find a problem in my logic. After a moment, he nodded, satisfied. "I like it. I like it a lot. Good work, investigator."

I felt warm with pride.

A rock-and-roll song played from the corner of the room. Vicente stood and headed for his phone, which was plugged into the wall.

I smirked. Of course he'd have AC/DC as his ringtone.

"Hello?" he answered in the honey-smooth voice he used to charm women. "Oh, hey Fred." The flirtation vanished from his tone. "Yeah, yeah. Oh, it wasn't a huge deal. I'd have gotten myself out with a few more minutes. Frannie might be exaggerating. You know how women are."

I openly rolled my eyes. At least a woman wouldn't crawl up into a giant piece of equipment without a plan and get herself trapped.

"Well, that's beside the point." Vicente sounded a little defensive, and I suspected Fred had scolded him for the sexist remark.

Score for Fred.

"Mmm-hmm," said Vicente. "Right, Kate told me the car should be ready tomorrow? Mechanic is ordering a part in?"

I couldn't make out Fred's reply. Swallowing, I eyed the plate of cookies again. *These are so deadly.* I'd gained a little more weight than I needed to this pregnancy, but . . . surely one more wouldn't hurt? I snatched another cookie and bit into it.

"Oh, that's great!" exclaimed Vicente, fist-pumping the air.

The man even looked dignified while fist-pumping. I devoured the cookie in two bites.

Maybe just one more?

No, Kate, I scolded myself. *You've had three cookies already—plus all the other food Gloria's plied you with.* To give my hands something to do that *wasn't* grabbing another cookie, I pulled a scrunchie out of my bag and threw my hopelessly frizzy hair into a messy bun.

"Wonderful," said Vicente. "I appreciate all you've done for us today. Yes, I can be ready in fifteen minutes." He set the phone down and walked back to the table. "The mechanic got a junk car in, and it has a part in good condition that's compatible with my car. It should be ready to roll within the hour—Fred's on his way here to pick me up."

Gloria poked her head out of the kitchen and gesticulated wildly, phone in hand—I caught a glimpse of Mom and Laurie still on videochat on her screen. "I can drive you, you know!" she called.

Vicente shrugged. "Well, Fred's already on the way."

Gloria *tsk*ed, but withdrew back into the kitchen, apologizing to Mom for the interruption. I got a chuckle out of it—it sounded like they were already fast friends.

"Do we know how to get in touch with Frannie?" I asked.

Vicente quirked his lips. "As a matter of fact, I have her number."

I tilted my head. "You do? How? You weren't even here!"

"I took her on a date three or four years back." He shrugged. "Sue me for being irresistible."

I scoffed. "I don't believe it. Have you taken every single woman in the world out on a date?"

"Only the pretty ones," he retorted.

"And you were so irresistible that she only went on one date with you?" I smirked.

He shifted uncomfortably. "I'd say it was more like we had a mutual sense it wasn't going to work out."

With a triumphant cackle, I cried, "She turned you down when you asked her for a second date! I can see it in your eyes!"

"Shut up," he muttered.

"Well, I'm glad to hear it." I readjusted my messy bun. "Because I liked Frannie very much, and for a moment there, I despaired of her sense of taste."

"Do you want me to call her or not?"

"No, I want to call her. She probably has your phone number listed under a contact called *SPAM*."

He shot me a withering look but retrieved his cell phone and read me the number. I dialed, and Frannie picked up on the third ring.

"Hello?" she said.

"Frannie, it's Kate Connolly, the private investigator?"

"You should introduce yourself as Kate Connolly, squirrel savior," she said, sounding cheerful but fatigued. "I got the little squirrel family to Maud, who was very impressed that you managed to save them from the fire. She said they look healthy—she'll keep them in a habitat for observation for a day or two, and if all looks well, she knows just how to release them back into the wild."

"I'm so glad to hear that!" I exclaimed.

"So, what's up? Were you calling to check on the squirrels, or do you need something?"

I held the phone between my shoulder and my ear and grabbed my pen. "I'm putting together a timeline of everyone's movements today and was wondering if you could help me out."

"Sure! Whatever I can do to be helpful."

"When you and Luz went to walk the grounds of the winery, were the two of you together the whole time?"

"Mmm, most of it," she said. "We went down to the grove by the lake and discussed what a reception would look like there. Oh, Kate! It'll be so beautiful." Her voice took on a dreamy tone, then she seemed to come back down to earth. "But right—timeline. So, we went there right after you left us. Luz had to run back to the house for a clipboard so she could take notes about the specifics. We were there until she got your text about Bruce, and then we ran to the bodega."

"How long was she gone for?"

"I'm not sure, exactly. Maybe fifteen minutes? She said she had trouble finding the clipboard."

CHAPTER 18

h-oh. The blood drained from my face. Frannie couldn't vouch for Luz's whereabouts the whole time. Fifteen minutes was a tight window for Luz to hit Bruce over the head, start a slow-burning fire, and produce a clipboard . . . but it wasn't impossible.

A prosecutor could claim with a straight face that it had happened that way.

"And what happened to the clipboard?" I asked. I closed my eyes and summoned the memory of the two of them running toward me at the scene. Luz hadn't been carrying a clipboard.

"Um . . ." She paused. "I'm not actually sure. I guess she probably brought it with her to the bodega? Or maybe she dropped it at the grove when we took off running?"

I struggled to keep my voice chipper and calm. "Well, thanks so much. That's very helpful for my timeline."

"Absolutely! Call back if you think of anything else. I might take a nap—it's been quite a day—but you're more than welcome to wake me up. Luz must be so angry about the fire."

I bit my lip. "Yeah, she's definitely angry. We're going to figure out who's responsible."

I couldn't make eye contact with Vicente when I hung up.

He finally broke the silence. "Luz and Frannie weren't together the whole time, I gather." Disappointment laced his voice. "So she doesn't have an alibi."

"Frannie says Luz was only gone for about fifteen minutes. That feels like a pretty tight time crunch to attack Bruce and start the fire."

"She left to do what?" he asked.

"Get a clipboard from the winery."

Vicente swore under his breath. "That awful detective will think fifteen minutes is a suspiciously long time to get a clipboard. The main building is only a two-minute walk from that grove."

Officer Stent's words replayed in my head. *We want to get to the truth, not just make an arrest and close the case. Well . . . at least that's what I want. Detective McNamara back there . . . he's running for sheriff in the next election.*

Luz needed an alibi so strong that Detective McNamara would realize his case against her couldn't possibly hold up. Even if it strained believability that she could have attacked Bruce at the bodega and set a fire in the vineyard in that amount of time . . . we needed more than that to combat Regina's claim that Bruce had identified Luz as the attacker.

"Then again," I murmured, "maybe we do need a fresh suspect list."

He reached for a cookie, and my mouth watered.

Okay, fine, just one more. I gave in and grabbed another one. I didn't even want to think about the number of calories I'd consumed today.

"What about security cameras?" I blurted.

Vicente snapped to attention. "There are a few around the property. Twenty years ago, my *abuelo* had them installed amid a string of break-ins in the area. Ordinarily, police would have collected the footage by now, but because of the fire . . ."

"There wasn't time to do that before everyone's attention was pulled away," I finished. "So they haven't done all of their normal investigation tactics yet."

He drummed his fingers on the table. "Let's go. There's a security room off the garage."

I followed him down a hall to the staircase that wound down to the basement garage. At the top of the stairs, I felt a little dizzy and gripped the handrail tightly. *One step at a time.*

We hit the bottom of the stairs, passed Luz's SUV, and walked through a nondescript door in the corner of the garage.

A bank of screens showed scenes from around the vineyard. I scowled at the TVs. "Why did no one tell me this was here when we were looking for you?"

He shrugged. "Guess they panicked?" He strode up to a keyboard, hit a few keys, and frowned. "Wait . . . what?"

"What's wrong?"

He reached out and stuck his hand into the VHS player, then swore under his breath. "There's no tape. We can see the live footage, but it's not writing a VHS tape. Did . . . did the saboteur steal them to hid his identity?"

Frantically, he began pawing through the shelf of VHS tapes.

"VHS tapes, huh?" I asked. "That's such old technology now. I'm amazed she can even find an inventory of those."

"They're labeled on the front with dates," he explained. After a couple minutes, he let out a long sigh. "No, not sabotage. Looks like Luz hasn't been making tapes for a couple months."

"She probably couldn't find any more to buy." I chewed my lip. "I guess that's why no one mentioned the cameras."

"Another dead end." His shoulders sagged. "I know it's all part of the job, but man . . . it feels different when it's your family member that police are treating like a suspect."

"I know," I murmured.

We slunk back to the kitchen table in disappointment, and I tried to suppress a horrible thought: Why would Luz have stopped recording security tapes when the vineyard was being sabotaged?

Could Regina Stringer and the investigating officer be right? Could Luz have us all fooled? It was hard for me to imagine that she'd been lying to me all day—I liked to think I had a decent read on people.

How will Vicente handle it if it turns out his beloved cousin is guilty?

I had to follow the truth, no matter where it led. But this felt agonizing to even consider.

When we returned, Gloria peered through the doorway at us. "Where were you?" she asked.

"Checking the security feeds," said Vicente. "But it looks like Luz stopped recording footage a couple months ago."

"Oh!" Gloria exclaimed. "After the burglary. No, she didn't stop the cameras. She's no *tonta*."

I exchanged a glance with Vicente.

Gloria continued, "After the burglary, Luz seemed . . . worried. More than made sense to me. It was just a burglary, I told her. It happened." She seemed thoughtful. "Now I understand. She'd been receiving those notes."

"So, what'd she do?" I asked.

Gloria crossed her arms. "She told me it was time to update to new technology. She got one of those fancy apps that connect to . . . thinking cameras."

"Smart cameras?" Vicente asked.

"Ah!" Gloria's face lit up. "Yes, that's what she called them. Smart cameras. She put one at the front and back of the house and another on the gravel road that goes into the vineyard fields. I think it sent a notification to her phone when there was movement. She had ordered a few more cameras with fancy features that she wanted to put around the rest of the vineyard, but they have not arrived yet—they were on backorder or something."

I snapped my fingers. "That's why she didn't tell me anything about the cameras. She gets a notification every time the camera sees anything—so she knew that it hadn't picked you up moving around the vineyard."

"Because she only had three cameras set up so far," said Vicente. "And after I left the wine cave, I didn't pass by any of them."

"Is her phone here?" I asked. "Or did she have it on her when she was arrested?"

"I'll call it!" Gloria grabbed her own phone and dialed.

We fell silent, listening for it to ring, but there was no response.

"What about her computer?" I finally asked. "Maybe we can log onto the video feed from there?"

"Her laptop is in her office, usually," said Gloria. "She keeps it hooked up there so she can use two computer screens."

Vicente shot to his feet and headed for the hallway. "I'll get it. Be right back."

While he was gone, I rubbed my temples and stared at my notes. What were we missing? Was there something obvious we weren't seeing?

A few moments later, Vicente returned, a silver laptop in hand.

"Is it password-protected?" I asked.

"Yeah, but I got in." He flashed a grin at me and set the laptop on the table. "The password was an inside joke."

He sank down onto the chair next to mine and opened Luz's email. "Okay . . ." he murmured as he typed. "Let's search for *smart camera*, maybe?"

A moment later, he had the brand of camera she'd ordered and had opened the website.

"She's logged in!" I exclaimed.

"Yup," he said, clicking through the website's menu. "Looks like we can't view the footage from here—that's probably for security reasons —but we can see the timestamps of when the camera picked up movement."

I glanced at my timeline and then pointed to a timestamp on the screen. "This must have been when she came back for the clipboard. She walked in the back door."

Vicente frowned as he skimmed the list. "This doesn't help us out, does it?"

My heart sank. He was right. The camera had detected movement at the back door four times in that fifteen-minute window. "Did she come in and out twice?" I asked.

"We won't know until we can look at the footage," said Vicente. "Maybe someone else came in and out? Or maybe a deer was wandering close enough to be picked up by the motion sensor?"

I let out a long sigh. "But the bottom line is that we don't have an alibi for her."

His lips tightened into a grim line. "No, we don't."

CHAPTER 19

*V*icente's phone blasted AC/DC, and he squirmed in his chair and glanced at the screen. "Hey, Fred," he answered, tapping the kitchen table with his free hand. "Perfect. I'll be out in a minute."

"Is that Fred?" called Gloria, walking into the room. "He's here? Tell him to come in for *polvorones de canele* before you drive into town. He's been a big help today."

With a shrug, Vicente said into the phone, "Fred, actually, why don't you come in the front? *Abuela* wants to force-feed you cookies." He stood and hung up. "I'll bring him back here."

When Vicente left, Gloria sat across the table from me. "You figured out how to help Luz?" she asked expectantly. "The cameras cleared her?"

I hesitated, and the hopeful expression on her face gave way to grief and concern. "No?"

"We weren't able to access the actual video footage," I said. "And the timestamps weren't definitive. But as soon as we can get hold of her phone and can see the video . . ."

"Luz will be okay?" Her questioning tone was like a knife in my gut.

I swallowed hard. Would the police even let us look through her phone? Or would they keep it as evidence? What if they never released the camera footage? Would we be able to prove Luz's innocence?

But I didn't want to let on that I was worried. "We're working on it from a couple angles," I said, projecting confidence. "And Gary is on his way here. She couldn't ask for a better defense attorney."

She nodded as if this satisfied her, but the fear didn't drain from her eyes.

My throat tickled, and a cough racked my body. *Guess my lungs are going to be irritated for a few days from that fire.*

Vicente and Fred strode into the room, and I gulped down water to quell my coughing fit.

"Do you think the owner needs a tow?" Fred was asking Vicente.

"I have no idea," he replied with a careless shrug.

"Huh." Fred's eyes narrowed in thought. "Kinda odd."

"Who needs a tow?" I asked.

"The white Prius out front." Vicente grabbed the plate of cookies and offered them to Fred.

Fred grabbed one and bit into it with an appreciative nod. "Gloria, these are excellent!"

Something churned in the back of my mind. *The white Prius out front.* There was something odd about that . . .

Gloria poked her head into the room and beamed at Fred. "I will send some *polvorones de canele* home for your little girl."

"Mighty thoughtful of you." He tipped his hat. "She's got a dangerous sweet tooth, that one!"

I've got one of those, too, I thought morosely, eyeing the plate of cookies and resisting a fifth helping of cinnamon-infused joy with every fiber of my being. *I'll have another cookie when I solve the case. That will be my reward.*

With a pang of sadness, I remembered the worry lines on Gloria's face. I so badly wanted to set her mind at ease. *I'll have a whole plate of cookies when I solve the case. And I won't even feel bad about it. So there.*

Then I forced myself back to the present. Back to the case. Back to the feeling that something was odd about . . .

"Wait," I said. "The white Prius is out front again? The same one that was here earlier?"

"Again?" Fred asked, his eyebrows knitting together. "Did it move? It's in the same spot it was when I was here before. And yeah—same car. Has a distinctive bumper sticker."

"Didn't the Prius belong to Regina's friend Alice?" I asked, glancing at Vicente.

"Um . . . I think that might have happened while I was"—he looked at Fred—"indisposed."

I snorted.

"Trapped in a fan with a squirrel?" Fred deadpanned. "Or are you still going to claim Frannie exaggerated that?"

"Anyway." Vicente enunciated each syllable. "The only white Prius *I* know of is the one that crazy lady owns, so I don't know anything about the car that's here."

I froze. *That crazy lady.*

The woman who'd found us stranded by the side of the road. I'd only seen the front of her car this morning, so I didn't know if it had any bumper stickers, but . . .

"Fred," I said. "Do you remember what bumper sticker was on her car?"

"It's a circle, with a picture of the world—like, a photo taken from space. The rim says, *I pledge allegiance to Mother Earth.*"

My gosh. It has to be her.

My voice took on new urgency. "The woman who called you to pick us up. Did she give you a name?"

"I think she did, actually. I can check my system." He pulled out his phone and tapped the screen a few times. "Um . . . looks like it was an Alice McCleary. I don't know who she is."

My jaw dropped.

He studied me. "That name means something to you, doesn't it?"

My mind raced, pieces of the puzzle clicking together. "It does. She's a close friend of Regina Stringer. She was here earlier . . . she and Regina were going to coffee. They were waiting for Fred. Regina was in the wine cave, and Alice decided to take a walk around the lake . . ."

Vicente pressed his palms together. "So, why is she back?"

I rubbed my temples, trying to think. "Regina said something earlier today. What . . ."

Then it hit me. I'd asked Regina if they'd told any rival vineyard owners about the reason Bruce was fired—about the counterfeit wine. She'd answered, *We complained about it to a couple close friends, but no—no one in the wine industry. People might misunderstand why Bruce did what he did, you know.*

Was one of those close friends Alice?

And if Alice was involved, was she acting alone, or were she and Regina in cahoots? I flipped back through my notepad, thankful I'd thought to get the contact information for my three early suspects.

"Wait, you think the crazy woman from this morning could be the saboteur?" Vicente asked. "But wasn't she late for her environmentalist meeting in Sacramento?"

I grabbed my phone. "Vicente, look up the information for the Sacramento Go-Green chapter, and see if you can contact them. We need to find out if Alice McCleary ever showed up at that meeting. I'm going to make another call." Quickly, I dialed Regina.

"Hello?" she answered.

"Regina, this is Kate Connolly. Are you still at the hospital?"

"Yes," she said, irritation coloring her voice.

"How's Bruce doing?"

"Still unconscious," she spat. "He woke up for a few moments earlier and said that Luz was the one who attacked him. I hope she's been arrested already."

Despite my flash of suspicion earlier and our inability to find Luz an alibi, I was pretty sure she hadn't attacked Bruce—and not just because she was Vicente's cousin and I liked her. It was more than that.

The story that implicated her didn't hold together in a way that made sense. Even *if* she were the sort of person who would risk starting a devastating wildfire—and I very much doubted she was—she wouldn't do it while her beloved cousin was missing on the property. Plus, if she wanted to collect insurance money, why make up a complicated story about ongoing sabotage? Why not set it up to look like an accident? Allegations of foul play would bring extra scrutiny, which an insurance fraudster wouldn't want.

So, was Bruce lying? Or confused? Or had Regina put words in his mouth?

"What exactly did Bruce say when he woke up?" I asked.

Out of the corner of my eye, I saw Vicente dialing a phone number.

"He told me who'd hit him over the head," Regina snapped in a shrill voice. "And that person was Luz."

CHAPTER 20

"*W*hat were Bruce's words verbatim?" I asked Regina, gripping the phone in white-knuckled fingers and trying to project patience through my voice.

Vicente walked across the room, speaking in soft tones on his phone.

She responded with a long-suffering sigh. "He opened his eyes and gasped. Then he said, '*Luz . . . danger . . . can't trust.*' And then he trailed off and fell unconscious again."

I blinked three times. She'd had Luz arrested over something as unspecific as *that*? "That's it? That's all he said?"

"Yes!" She sounded like she was close to tears. "What do you mean, *that's all he said*? He said her name! She attacked him!"

I grabbed hold of an idea—a way to test the evidence. "Of course. I'm so sorry. Yes, Luz has been arrested. Did you call in an anonymous tip?"

She paused, and I listened carefully to the tenor of her voice. "What?" she asked.

Confusion, I decided. She was confused by my question. I didn't reply, just waited for her to elaborate.

"No," she said finally. "I wasn't anonymous. I gave them my name. Did they not write that down? I told them I was Bruce's wife, that I was calling from the hospital, and that he'd woken up and named Luz as his attacker."

"Okay," I said. "Maybe I just misunderstood the police. Everything happened so fast, you know."

Maybe Regina was just a good actress, but my gut told me she hadn't expected my question. And if that proved true, if I had a good read on her, it meant she hadn't called in the anonymous tip about the insurance fraud.

Vicente returned to the table and sat down, shoving his phone in his pocket.

I took a deep breath and focused on my conversation with Regina. "To tell you the truth, I'm starting to suspect you might have been right about the insurance fraud angle that you mentioned at the hospital."

"Oh?" Again, she sounded surprised.

Vicente crossed his arms and stared at me, but I just smiled back at him mysteriously.

"Can I ask you what led you to suspect that?" I continued. "I can't tell Vicente this, of course—he absolutely believes in Luz's innocence—but I want to chase down that lead and see what I can dig up."

"Um . . ." Her voice softened. "Sure. Sorry, I guess I just assumed you were Team Luz because she hired you to investigate us and because you're friends with Vicente."

"It's like I said earlier, I'm Team Truth," I replied. "I didn't have a reason to suspect Luz when we talked before, but as a matter of principle, I follow the evidence wherever it leads me."

Vicente's lips formed a thin line, and I rolled my eyes at him.

"Don't worry," I mouthed.

"Well," Regina said, grabbing my attention. "I was talking the whole situation over with a friend—before I found out Bruce was hurt."

"With Alice, was it?" I asked. "While you were still at the vineyard?"

"Yeah. She thought Luz's allegations against Bruce and me sounded really weird. Said it almost sounded like Luz was laying the groundwork for us to take the fall for something. Something bad."

My heart beat faster. "And Alice knew why Bruce had been fired? That's why she suspected Luz was planning something."

"Exactly! Oh, it relieves me so much that you think this all sounds reasonable."

"So," I said slowly. "That's why you were suspicious Luz was up to something. What made you think insurance, specifically? Could you be as detailed as possible? That will help with my investigation."

"Well, I'm not sure I have anything concrete, but I'll do my best. When I was at Bruce's bedside, Alice called me, out of breath. First, she asked how Bruce was—she was very relieved he was okay. Then she explained there was a fire at the vineyard and she'd had to run to her car and gun it to get out of there."

One line stood out to me: *First, she asked how Bruce was.*

How had Alice known Bruce was hurt? We hadn't told her—we hadn't even talked to her before she left the property. Had Fred or Officer Anderson run into her and explained the situation?

"Anyway," Regina continued. "I asked her to go to our house and load our two horses into the trailer and drive them to Bruce's mom's ranch an hour north, so she's doing that right now. Before she hung up, she muttered something like, *I knew Luz was planning something.* And I just knew. The only reason I can think of that Luz would have started that fire was for insurance money." Then she paused. "Oh! I guess maybe she could have done it to cover up her murder of Bruce—I'm sure she thought he was dead when she left him there. That's really all I know. I'm sorry—as I say it out loud, I realize it's probably not very helpful from an investigation stand-point. But thank you for taking me seriously. I'm so glad you're looking into it."

"Well, thank you anyway." I drummed my pen on the table. "If you think of anything else, or if Bruce wakes up again, please give me a call."

I hung up.

Vicente said, "I got in touch with the chair of the Sacramento chapter of Go-Green. Alice McCleary was supposed to be there today to present a plan for a fundraiser. She never showed. Sent one text saying she was running late, and then twenty minutes later, called him and said something had come up and she couldn't make it. He thought she sounded agitated."

Tense silence lingered in the air.

"Fred," I said finally. "After you stayed behind to give your statement to the police officer, did you run into a heavyset blonde by any chance?"

"No, ma'am." He shook his head thoughtfully. "I didn't see anyone else before I left. Why?"

I sat in silent concentration for a moment.

"Kate," interjected Vicente. "What are you thinking? How does it all fit together?"

"Alice McCleary knew why Bruce had been fired, *and* she put the insurance fraud story in Regina's head. She was on the property, conveniently taking a walk around the lake by herself, when Bruce was attacked and the fire started. And"—I paused for dramatic effect—"she called to ask Regina how Bruce was doing, even though none of us talked to her and told her Bruce had been hurt."

Fred whistled. "Well, that's mighty suspicious."

One more thing churned in the back of my mind. "Oh! Frannie said that Alice is a literature professor. At the community college."

Vicente and Fred looked at me expectantly.

I waved wildly at Vicente. "The notes! The literary allusions! It all makes sense!"

He squinted. "Why the obvious errors in the notes?"

"Errors?" Fred asked.

"Spelling," I replied. "*Your* versus *you're*, apostrophes, that sort of thing."

"Maybe she was throwing off suspicion?" Fred said. "She couldn't help but work in the literature references, so she made errors that she wouldn't ordinarily make."

I fired off a text to Officer Stent, asking if he'd made contact with anyone fitting Alice's description. "I have one more person I need to double-check with . . ."

A moment later, the reply arrived.

No, Officer Stent wrote. *After I debriefed Fred, I saw the smoke, radioed it in, and went to the scene to monitor it until the fire department reached the scene. Didn't see anyone else on the property, sorry. You have a lead?*

I shot back another text. *Working on one.* Then I set the phone down and said, "Officer Stent didn't tell Alice that Bruce had been attacked, either. Which means—"

Vicente snapped his fingers. "She had no way of knowing he was hurt, unless—"

In unison, Fred and I said, "She attacked him."

"Motive?" Vicente asked. "I want to make sure this is rock-solid."

The doorbell rang. Vicente stood to head out and answer it, but Gloria shuffled past him.

"I will get it!" she declared, waving us back to the table. "You are making progress. Focus on helping Luz."

Vicente steepled his fingers, and Fred leaned forward.

"Motive," I said. "So, after that phone conversation I just had, I don't think Regina is involved. She wouldn't have given me all those details if she'd had any inkling that Alice was the culprit."

"What if she sensed that we were closing in and decided to throw Alice under the bus?" Vicente asked. "Or maybe attacking Bruce was never part of the plan, and she wanted to make Alice pay for hurting her husband?"

"No." Fred peered intently at my page of notes. "If she conspired with Alice, the evidence is out there. Their only hope of self-preservation would be to back up each other's stories."

If Fred wasn't an undercover cop, like Luz half-suspected, he should be—he had a great eye for detail and a sharp analytical mind.

"Suspects don't always think clearly," said Vicente. "Especially when things get out of hand. And this clearly got out of hand."

I massaged my forehead. "But I think Fred's right. Regina doesn't strike me as a carefully controlled person."

"That's fair," Vicente conceded.

I flipped back a couple pages. "She flew off the handle and confronted Luz because she suspected Luz and Bruce were having an affair . . . because Bruce was working late during a period when the winery was in crisis. And Bruce told Luz this wasn't the first time Regina had done that sort of thing. Plus, when Luz and I were at the hospital, Regina basically told us she was going to libel Luz to the newspapers. That's not something you say strategically—it gave us a heads-up that we could have used to hire a lawyer or go to the press ourselves and preempt the story."

"She doesn't hide her emotions, or think before she speaks," Vicente said slowly. "With a person like that, more often than not, what you see is what you get."

"It's a character trait that makes her volatile." Fred reached for a cookie. "But actually gives her less ability to master-plan something like this."

"So." I stared at the plate in the middle of the table. There was one *polvorone de canele* left. My mouth watered. It did *seem* like I'd just cracked the case. I snatched the cookie.

The door to the apartment swung open, but I kept my attention fixed on Fred and Vicente.

"Let's assume Alice was working alone," I said. "The motive must have been revenge—she was angry on Bruce's behalf and set out to teach Luz a lesson."

Vicente squinted at me. "If this was all about how much she cared about Bruce and Regina, why would she have attacked Bruce?"

"You're all wrong!" a woman shrieked.

As one, Vicente, Fred, and I swung to face the voice. Shock and fear rippled through my body, and I dropped the *polvorone de canele* to the floor.

Alice McCleary stood in the doorway, holding a knife to Gloria's throat.

CHAPTER 21

"*E*asy, there, Alice." I held up my hands, hoping to calm her. "Don't do anything rash. It'll only make things worse for you."

Her eyes bulged, a crazed light dancing in their depths. Gloria stood there, frozen.

Bile scalded my throat, and I swallowed it back. We needed to defuse the situation and get the knife away from Alice before she hurt Gloria . . . and before the stress of the situation sent Gloria into a full-on heart attack.

"Listen," I said. "Let Gloria go, and tell us where we're wrong. We'll help you figure out what to tell the cops and make sure you have a good defense attorney. No one's died . . . and your cooperation will go a long way toward getting you a good plea deal or making you sympathetic to a jury."

"I didn't mean to hurt Bruce," Alice spat, visibly trembling.

I blanched. Maybe Alice hadn't *meant* to hurt Bruce, but she had. Now, she was shaking while holding a knife to an old woman's throat. Would she hurt Gloria without *meaning* to?

We couldn't afford to take that chance.

Then Alice's gaze hardened. "But, once I did, I didn't feel too bad about it. Really, he deserved it. But I didn't realize it was Bruce when I swung the shovel. I thought you"—she stared in unbridled rage at Vicente—"were snooping around and found me."

"Ah, so you only meant to hurt me, then," Vicente muttered. "So much better."

I gave Alice a soft smile, hoping to quell her insane anger. "Why did Bruce deserve it?" I asked. "He must have done something terrible."

Vicente grumbled under his breath, but I ignored him. I'd charmed Alice once before. I just needed to do it again.

But now the stakes were so much higher.

Alice barked with laughter. "I tried to get Bruce to leave that toxic industry so many times over the years, and he wouldn't. When Luz fired him, I thought it would finally happen. He'd join the side of the angels—or at least leave the side of the demons."

"The wine industry?" I asked, keeping a close watch on the knife in her hand. "It's toxic?"

She bristled. "You don't know that? It takes so much land and water and fossil fuels—all to produce a poison people can drink to numb themselves from the world's problems. Booze keeps people in a stupor, pacifies them so they don't actually *do* things to save the planet. Do you know what color polish Regina got at that stupid manicure?"

My mind stuttered, trying to make sense of the quick change in topics. "Um . . . green, wasn't it? Like, neon?"

"Yeah," she snorted. "As green as toxic waste. And you know what she said to me when I met her here?"

"What?"

Her face scrunched up, and she affected a mocking imitation of Regina's voice, "Oh, Alice, look—don't you love my nails? They're green, like all of your causes!" She shook her head, her voice returning to normal. "Those people are so clueless. I don't know why I was friends with them for so many years." Then she laughed. "Not friends with them anymore, I guess. Good riddance."

Her careless tone sent chills down my spine.

"Help me understand," I said slowly, keeping my hands up in a nonthreatening manner. "Why target Luz? Why send those notes? Why the cyberattack?"

Alice blinked a few times. "Luz is one of the bad guys. She's part of that toxic industry. Don't you understand? You're pregnant—don't you want a better future for your baby, like you said in the car this morning?"

I rested a hand on my abdomen and glanced at Gloria. Though she still looked alarmed, she didn't seem to be in pain—which meant the knife wasn't digging into her skin. "Of course I do. I just want to know—why Luz specifically? Why Luz, out of all the winery owners in the area? Did she do something to especially deserve it?"

Alice froze for a moment, confusion flickering over her face. "Well, she fired Bruce."

Tilting my head, I said, "But I thought you decided you hated Bruce."

"Well." She managed a shrug. "I didn't decide that until today. Regina and Bruce talked and talked and talked about how much Luz had betrayed them. Plus, they lived nearby and knew the vineyard so well, and Bruce had always talked about his work. So I knew about a lot of the operation already. I brought over a couple bottles of wine one night and let Bruce vent all his revenge fantasies. It didn't take much prodding to draw more specifics out of him—where the cameras were, what kind of computer system Luz had."

"Smart," I replied. "You did your research on your target."

She smirked. "Bruce has worked in the wine industry for all these years and bragged about his tolerance for that poison. He was so confused the next day when he couldn't remember what we'd talked about. Kept asking how he'd managed to get blackout drunk. Never even suspected that I'd laced the wine."

I ran my hand up and down my baby bump for effect and let tears brim in my eyes. "I understand what you did," I said softly. "I don't condone the methods, but the world's such a terrible place. At least you did something to try to make it better."

"See!" She pulled the knife from Gloria's throat and gestured in triumph toward me. "I knew you'd understand." Though she still had a tight grip on the old woman's shoulder, she didn't put the knife back against her neck. "After we talked this morning, I couldn't get the conversation out of my head. Plus, I knew the stupid detective cousin coming into town meant I had to act fast—he might put a stop to my plan. So I decided to not go to my meeting—that I needed to accelerate my plan instead."

I took a tentative step forward, one hand still raised, the other cradling my babies. "But the fire, Alice? All that smoke in the atmosphere? The animals that got caught up in it? What if the fire department hadn't been able to put it out, and the whole area had a wildfire? I almost died saving a squirrel nest!"

A look of guilt crossed her face. "I didn't mean to kill any animals, or for the fire to get out of control like that. You've got to believe me. I left Regina in the wine cave—told her I was taking a walk—and then grabbed the shovel out of my car. I was going to go dig up some of the grapevines."

"And then Bruce surprised you. That's why you hit him."

"I thought it was Luz's stupid cousin," she exclaimed.

I took another small step toward her, my heart beating more quickly. I had to knock the knife out of her hands so she couldn't hurt Gloria. But the idea of lunging at her—of putting my babies in danger again—sent hot fear hurtling through my body.

"Once I hit him," she continued, "I tried to figure out what to do. Went through his pockets and took his wallet and his lighter to make it look like a robbery. I thought about hitting him again to make sure he was really dead, but I had a hard time making myself do it. Then I heard you on the path, and I dropped the shovel and scurried back into the bushes to hide. You called the cops, and I knew I was screwed. The cops would want to talk to everyone who'd been on the property, and I'm bad at hiding things once people start asking me questions."

That's for sure, I thought.

"But I had Bruce's lighter, so I beat it out to the vineyard and set a few grapevines on fire. Figured that would distract the cops long enough for me to drive off—plus, no one could fault me for running away from a fire. If they remembered to question me later, I'd at least have bought myself time to rehearse my story." She whistled. "The grapevines lit up like fireworks. Wasn't expecting them to burn so bright so fast."

"Of course you weren't," I said soothingly, taking another step forward.

"And now I'm caught!" she cackled. "When I decided to take out the winery, I secretly installed an app on Regina and Bruce's phones that let me listen to their conversations. So I heard your whole little chat with Regina, and it was obvious you'd figured it out. Figured I might as well come here and give you my side of the story—you and I saw eye-to-eye about that stupid car, so I thought you might understand why I had to do it."

I took a deep breath. It was now or never. I had to get the knife away from Alice. One more step. "Of course—"

A blur of motion and muscle surged past me. In one fluid move, Fred struck Alice's hand, sending the knife hurtling across the room. Then he grabbed her shoulder, pushing her back away from Gloria.

I jolted forward, put my arm around Gloria and ushered the old woman away. Vicente appeared at our side, taking his *abuela* by the arm and helping her to a seat at the table.

"*Abuela*, are you all right?" he asked, his face white.

She nodded fiercely. Though she was pale, her lips curled into a triumphant grin. "Luz! We can prove it wasn't Luz!"

Vicente let out a deep breath, almost a chuckle, and held up his phone. "We sure can. The second that hag started singing about her crimes, I started recording. We've got it all on tape."

Alice screamed, jerking my attention away. She was sitting on the ground, with Fred kneeling behind her, pinning her arms.

"Someone call the cops here to pick her up," called Fred. "And could someone get the zip ties out of my truck? They're in the big toolbox."

"I'll get them," I said, so Vicente could stay with his *abuela*.

"I'll call 911," added Vicente.

Five minutes later, a red-faced Alice was zip-tied in the corner, and the police were on their way.

Officer Stent was first on the scene. We led him to collect Alice, and he studied her skeptically.

"Well, Kate," he said, pulling out his handcuffs and a pocketknife. "You work fast, but I hope you had a very good reason to detain the suspect by force."

"Citizen's arrest," Vicente interjected. "She took my *abuela* hostage and held a knife to her throat. I told the 911 dispatcher all that."

Officer Stent looked at me, and I nodded.

"Well, in that case, sounds like you were fully justified. It'll just be a little more paperwork." He handcuffed a spitting Alice, then cut the zip-ties off her hands and feet. "Alice McCleary, you have the right to remain silent. Anything you say can and will be used against you in a court of law."

Two paramedics rushed in, and we directed them to Gloria—just to be on the safe side. More officers flowed into the room, including Detective McNamara, the officer who'd been so enthusiastic about arresting Luz.

I marched up to him. "I'd like to give a statement," I said. "And I want to thank Officer Stent for his hard work on this case. He's a great cop and was very helpful."

He scowled at me, then pulled out his recording device and notepad. "Of course I'll take your statement," he muttered.

I decided right then and there that I was going to sing Officer Stent's praises to the local news station, too—so this ambitious wannabe politician couldn't take credit for the case.

For a moment, my mind flashed to Sergeant McNearny, my long-time nemesis back in the San Francisco Police Department. He and I clashed on almost every case I worked, but I realized with a rush of gratitude that, in reality, he couldn't be more different from this Detective McNamara. For all McNearny's bluster, he wanted the truth —he didn't just want to make an arrest to fill a quota. He didn't like it when I intruded on his turf, but he was a good cop, devoted to his job, committed to serve and protect.

I'd try to be nicer to McNearny the next time he and I went toe to toe.

Maybe.

When I finished telling the story, I waved Vicente over to play the audio recording.

"Well," said Detective McNamara, rubbing the back of his neck. "Good work. I'll radio back to the station and have them start processing Luz Barramendi for release."

"No need!" declared Luz, striding into the room alongside a tall, gangly figure in jeans and a button-up.

"Gary!" I cried, grinning at the gangly man. I glanced at my watch. "That was fast."

"Drove like a maniac to be here for my sister," he said, shooting a cold look at Detective McNamara. "But seems like I had no cause to worry—you two already wrapped up the case?"

"Taped confession and everything," said Vicente, high-fiving him.

"Dream team." Barramendi crossed his arms and nodded approvingly. "San Francisco's finest PIs."

Luz looped her arm through Barramendi's. "They're bigger than just San Francisco now. We should call them California's finest PIs."

I couldn't help but stand a little taller at the compliment.

"Luzita!" Gloria cried. She shoved the paramedics aside and ran to her granddaughter. "Oh, and Gary! You're here! My grandchildren!" She pulled Luz, Vicente, and Barramendi into a group hug. Then she drew back, a tender look on her face. "My legacy."

Tears brimmed in Luz's eyes. She sat down at the table, motioning Gloria to sit next to her. "*Abuela*, I . . . I have something to confess to you. About the winery."

She poured out the story—about the harvest, about Bruce and the counterfeit wine, about the award and the newspaper coverage, and finally, about the sabotage.

Even though Gloria had heard most of this from Vicente already, she listened and nodded, smiling compassionately. When Luz finished, the old woman reached out and grabbed her hand. "Why didn't you tell me, Luzita?"

"Your doctor said you needed to avoid stress, that your heart—"

Gloria looked as regal as a queen, but with the softness of silk. "Luzita," she cooed. "I am always here for my family. No matter what."

Luz wiped tears from her eyes. "And you and *abuelo* worked so hard to make Castillo's what it is." A little sob wracked her body. "It's your legacy."

"No, *nieta.*" Gloria pulled Luz into an embrace, comforting her like she was a small child. "Castillo's was our livelihood. A place we loved in many ways. A place we built, yes. But not our legacy. You—you are my legacy. You, and your brother, and Vicente, and all my children and grandchildren."

Sobs convulsed Luz's body.

The twins moved, sending a fluttering feeling through my core, and I realized I was crying. "You're my legacy," I whispered to them. "The two of you and your big sister, Laurie. Even more than these cases I'm solving—although those are important, too."

Intense homesickness washed over me. *Must be the pregnancy hormones. I haven't even been gone overnight.*

But all at once, I wanted nothing more than to go home.

CHAPTER 22

"*H*oney, I'm proud of you, but please never risk your life to save a *squirrel* again." Jim and I were sitting on opposite ends of the couch, facing each other, our legs intertwined. I was propped up with pillows, my precious baby girl napping in the crook of my arm.

Together again at last.

I'd taken a couple days to rest and recover from the adventure in Golden and had finally confessed the squirrel incident to Jim.

"But they're so cute!" I said, holding out my phone to show him a video that Maud the wildlife rehabilitator had sent me. It showed the baby squirrels tumbling over each other in a tiny habitat. "She says she going to release them back into the forest tomorrow."

"Honey, I'm serious," he insisted.

Our almost-full-grown tabby cat leaped onto his lap and rubbed her chin against his hand. "Yeah," Jim cooed to her. "You'd like to eat those squirrels, huh?"

I laughed aloud. "I'll try not to do anything like that again. But Jim, you just don't understand the way she looked at me. The way she asked for help, from one mom to another."

"Darling!" Mom swept into the living room from the kitchen, carrying a plate. "I think I've got it right!"

She held out the *polvorones de canele* to Jim, then me. I took a bite with a happy sigh. "Mmm! Yes, these are perfect!"

Whiskers's ears perked up, and she looked hopefully at Jim. He chuckled and broke off a tiny piece for her. She sniffed it, then wrinkled her nose and jumped off his lap.

"Oh, is this the recipe Vicente's grandmother gave you, Vera?" Jim asked. "Man, Kate wasn't kidding about how good these are."

"Absolutely deadly," I replied.

"It is." Mom set the plate on the coffee table and grabbed two cookies. "She and I have swapped a few recipes now."

I suppressed a grin. Mom had *definitely* gotten the better end of that deal. I tried to imagine Gloria making some hideous Jell-O concoction at Mom's recommendation.

Nope, couldn't picture it. Gloria had better sense than that, surely.

"In fact." She gesticulated wildly with a cookie in each hand. "I really want to try making Spanish tortillas for you. How about Sunday brunch?"

"Homemade tortillas?" Jim asked, brow furrowed. "Like, for brunch? I guess we could bring some breakfast burrito fillings."

Mom and I laughed, and I said, "No need. You'll understand when we have brunch. It's a very different kind of tortilla."

Mom's phone chimed. "Oh, that's a videocall," she said. She pulled out her phone and brightened when she saw the screen. "Oh! It's Gloria! Speaking of these cookies." She answered the phone. "Gloria!"

"*Hola*, Vera!" cried Gloria. "Did the *polvorones de canele* turn out?"

Mom held a cookie up to the camera. "They're absolutely divine. Can't thank you enough for this recipe. I have one for a Jell-O tiramisu if you'd like."

Jim and I smirked at each other, and I called, "Gloria! How are Luz and Vicente doing?"

Mom turned the screen around so Gloria and I could see each other.

Gloria beamed. "I'm so glad to see you home with your babies! Gary drove safely home?"

"Absolutely." I'd hitched a ride back to San Francisco with Barramendi—he'd needed to get back to his clients, and Vicente had wanted to spend a little more time with his family.

Gloria turned her head to speak in hushed tones with someone, and then Luz's face appeared on the screen.

"Kate!" Luz cried. "It's so good to see you."

"How are you holding up?"

"Great, now that no one's accusing me of attempted murder," she said with a wry chuckle.

"How's Bruce doing? Is he out of the hospital yet?"

"He was just released. He'll need some physical therapy, but he should be all right. Turns out he hadn't meant to accuse me—he knew it was Alice, but he only got a few words out the first time he woke up, and Regina misinterpreted them."

"Fancy that," I said dryly. "I can't imagine Regina jumping to conclusions about something."

Laurie stirred and let out a tired cry, and Mom pulled the phone back and walked into the kitchen to talk more with Gloria.

I smiled indulgently at my baby girl and offered her a tiny bite of cookie. "Want some cinnamon sugar, little duck?"

She opened her mouth, and I plopped the scrumptious morsel in. She paused, then her eyes widened and she reached out her hand for more. We ate our way through three cookies, then Mom returned and snatched the plate away.

"For your own good," she called, disappearing into the kitchen. "Or Laurie will get sugar-hyper, and you're still exhausted from your last adventure."

I stretched, then shifted Laurie onto my lap. "Could we take a walk down at Ocean Beach?"

"Are you sure?" Jim asked. "The sun just set, and it's supposed to be foggy this evening. Probably pretty chilly by the water."

Foggy, chilly San Francisco. Just the way I liked it. "Even better!" I declared. "You have no idea how hot and miserable I was in Golden. We'll bundle up."

"I'll see if Galigani wants to join us!" Mom yelled.

I heaved myself to my feet, groaning, and one of the twins started playing soccer against my bladder.

"Hey, stop it," I scolded, pressing a hand to my abdomen. "I'm about ready for you two to make your big debut, you know."

Jim laughed and scooped Laurie up. "They'll be here soon, huh? Hard to believe we'll be a family of five!"

A family of five.

Love and joy swelled in my chest. I grabbed my husband's collar and pulled him close—or as close as I could with Laurie and the baby bump between us.

Jim leaned down and kissed me breathless, and everything in the world seemed right. When he broke away, he whispered, "This is going to be the best of adventures."

<><><>

Thank you for reading CEREAL KILLER! I hope you love Kate and her family as much as I do. If you can't wait to read more MATERNAL INSTINCTS MYSTERIES, then keep in touch and let me know! **www.dianaorgain.com**

IF YOU LOVED THE TOWN OF GOLDEN, THERE'S MORE TO THE STORY...

WELCOME TO GOLDEN...WHERE MURDER AND SCANDAL RUN AS DEEP AS THE *gold mines....*

ONE-CLICK THE **GOLD STRIKE MYSTERIES** HERE!

IF YOU LOVED MY MATERNAL INSTINCTS MYSTERIES, YOU'LL love the fast-paced fun of **A FIRST DATE WITH DEATH**. Some are in it for love . . . others for the cash. Georgia just wants to stay alive . . .

. . .

AND DON'T MISS MY **YAPPY HOUR** SERIES. IT'S SWEET AND FUNNY and you'll laugh out loud as Maggie, not quite a dog lover, hunts down a murderer. Will Maggie's investigation kill her budding romance with Officer Brooks?

AND IF YOU'RE LOOKING FOR SOMETHING MAGICAL, TRY **A WITCH CALLED WANDA**. Will fledging witch Maeve reverse the curse that has Chuck doomed to live the rest of his days as a female dog . . . or will someone get away with murder?

SIGN UP AT MY **WWW.DIANAORGAIN.COM** TO FIND OUT ABOUT NEW releases and for exclusive sneak peeks of future books. I appreciate your help in spreading the word about my books, including telling a friend. Reviews help readers find books! Please leave a review on your favorite book site.

PREVIEW OF DYING FOR GOLD

CHAPTER 1

"*J*think your store is haunted," Mrs. Jeffries, one of our best customers, screeched.

"It's not haunted," I said.

"Well, the nugget I was just looking at disappeared out from under my nose! How do you explain that?" she demanded.

"Wendy," I offered as way of explanation, pulling the diamond-encrusted gold nugget out of my sister-in-law's hands and passing it to Mrs. Jeffries.

Wendy simply batted her false eyelashes and gave a wicked grin. "I couldn't resist. Isn't it the most amazing thing you've ever seen?"

The store in question was *The Nugget*. Daddy's family had been part of the original gold rush of 1849. Our family went way back, especially by California standards. I was the fifth generation of a mining family, and *The Nugget* had kept our family in gold even when our mine, *The Bear Strike*, had been forced to close in 1942 to support the war effort.

I don't know that I've ever seen Daddy happier than when the price of gold shot up a few years back and it would finally be profitable to reopen the mine.

Ordinarily, *The Nugget* catered to tourists, but I'd convinced Daddy to use the shop as a backdrop to put my best friend, Ginger's, exquisite jewelry designs on display, and all our best customers and neighbors had come out for the occasion.

Dad came around from behind the counter. "Cut the champagne off," he said under his breath.

I laughed. "Daddy! This is a ladies' gathering. One of the main draws beside Ginger's designs is the champagne."

He leaned into me. "Key word being *ladies*. Do you see how they're acting?"

I couldn't deny that there was a lot of shrieking going on and that the general timbre in the room was reaching an ear-shattering pitch. "You're just mad that they're so excited about Ginger's design and not your gold," I teased.

Dad's idea of jewelry was literally a nugget hanging off a chain, and the chain, of course, must be gold. There was nothing more appealing to him. The rougher the nugget, the more gorgeous Dad thought it was. I had to admit that our regular clientele of tourists seemed to agree.

They loved buying a "gen-u-ine" gold nugget that had been mined from California's oldest and still active mines.

Ginger came out of the back room cradling a sapphire necklace she'd taken to fix that'd been broken a moment earlier when two customers yanked it out of each other's hands. The pendant of the necklace was designed as a huge calla lily with delicate gold leaves and a brilliant-cut sapphire as the blossom. The necklace was almost as beautiful as Ginger herself.

She had honey-ginger colored hair and wore a form-fitting dress that hugged every generous curve. The dress was indigo, and knowing Ginger, it was no coincidence that it perfectly matched both her eyes and the expensive sapphire she now held in her hand.

She stood between the customers, Mrs. DeLeon and Mrs. Harvey, nervously glancing at me. "Uh, Frannie? Can you—"

"It's for me," Mrs. DeLeon said, grabbing at her pocketbook.

"No. You. Don't!" Mrs. Harvey howled. "That piece is for me. Wendy and I have been talking about it for ages!"

All heads turned toward my sister-in-law, Wendy, who dutifully wrinkled her button nose, then admitted, "I did tell her I thought there was a special piece she would like." Wendy avoided Mrs. Harvey's wrath by taking great interest in the passing waiter. "Oooh! Is that pâté?"

We'd hired an upscale catering service, *Bites & Bread*, for the event, and judging by the trays being offered to our customers, I could already hear Dad complain about the bill that was sure to be anything but *bite*-size.

However, he hadn't really had a choice. The competitor caterer was *Golden Grub*, run by mother and after their horrible divorce, Dad would rather stick himself in the eye with hot pokers than give my mother any business. Plus, he'd said over and over that Mom was just waiting for her moment to poison him...given their animosity I couldn't blame him.

The waiter, who was about all of eighteen, held the tray out for Wendy as Mrs. Harvey took a great inhale, then puffed out her cheeks. She let the air out slowly, breathing all over the canapé tray.

"I'm going to have to speak to Mr. Peterson! George!" she wailed.

Dad appeared with a smile on his face. He was ever the charmer, but I could tell by the fine lines around his eyes that he was tired. One more complaint from the wealthy, pampered socialites this party had attracted and he might blow a gasket.

"Mrs. Harvey. Whatever is the matter? More champagne?" he offered.

I bit back my laugh.

So much for cutting off the champagne!

"George. Will you please inform Mrs. DeLeon that the sapphire necklace is for me?"

Dad grabbed the arm of another waiter, this one a redhead who worked regularly at the *Bites & Bread Bakery*, and pulled a bottle of champagne out of her hand. He topped off Mrs. Harvey's glass. "Sapphire?" He frowned. "Mrs. Harvey. You and I must have a talk." He glanced around, all the ladies suddenly craning their necks to get an earful. "In private," he mumbled, leading her toward the glass case that held our most expensive gold jewelry.

Dad handed me the champagne bottle, then took Mrs. Harvey's elbow, leading her to the back of the store as he chatted with her, tilting his head close to hers so his mouth was near her ear. She suddenly erupted into a fit of giggles, then whacked my father on his shoulder. I noticed her hand lingered on his arm, giving him the occasional squeeze.

Didn't she realize she was the one being squeezed?

Mrs. DeLeon said, "Quick, Frannie. Ring me up for the sapphire necklace so I can get out of here and away from Mrs. Harvey."

I topped off Mrs. DeLeon's flute. "I think she'll change her mind altogether about the necklace. Don't worry."

Mrs. DeLeon handed me her platinum American Express. "I'm not taking any chances."

I took the card and nodded. "It is a beautiful piece. I'm sure you'll be very happy with it."

Ginger beamed as I rang up the necklace. "I can't believe this is happening. Everyone loves my stuff."

"I knew they would. It's beautiful," I said.

Wendy slipped up next to us. "Totally unique," she agreed. "I'm so glad I convinced George to have the party. What a great idea I had!"

Ginger and I exchanged a look. Actually, the idea of hosting an exclusive sale of Ginger's handcrafted designer jewelry had been mine, but we both knew Wendy would take credit wherever she could get it.

I rang up Mrs. DeLeon and placed the beautiful sapphire necklace into a black velvet gift box.

Wendy and Ginger circulated around the crowd, and Dad popped open another champagne bottle while chatting with Mrs. Harvey.

As I finished helping Mrs. DeLeon, she leaned in and grabbed my hand. "When are we going to see a ring on this finger, Frannie?"

I flushed. For some reason, I hated being the center of attention. I'd much rather people notice the sparkling gold nuggets beneath the glass counter than my hand above it.

"It's getting to be about that time, isn't it, dear?" Mrs. DeLeon asked.

I slipped my hand out of her grasp and feigned a smile. Even though I was hoping for a proposal soon, I wasn't about to share the details of my private life. "When he's ready, I'll be ready," I said.

Mrs. DeLeon gave a throaty chuckle. "Well, my dear, don't wait too long. I know your father is dying for some grandbabies to help out with *The Bear Strike*. Speaking of grandbabies, where did Wendy fly off to?" Mrs. DeLeon turned to look for Wendy.

Oh, good. She could go bug Wendy about getting pregnant soon and that would get me off the hook for the moment.

"Over there," I said, pointing toward Wendy's slender form. "No baby bump yet . . ."

Wendy turned toward me as if she'd sensed we were talking about her. I winked and wiggled my eyebrows, indicating that Mrs. DeLeon was about to descend on her.

She gave me her best "you'll pay for this" look, then smiled as Mrs. DeLeon approached.

I took the opportunity to slip to the back and dial my boyfriend, Jason. We'd been dating for almost a year, and he'd recently been hinting around the idea of marriage, asking my ring size and whether I preferred white gold or yellow.

Which actually was a silly question for a gold heiress. While gold could be many colors, including black or purple, nothing compared to those flakes colored like the sun. But hey, if being agreeable to pink or red gold would get a ring on my finger, I was all for it.

In fact, Jason had been mysterious about this evening. He'd mentioned a romantic dinner and a *surprise*.

I dialed his number and waited for him to answer. It rang four times, and then his voicemail kicked on.

Where was he?

It wasn't like him not to pick up.

Maybe he's shopping.

I imagined him haggling with a jeweler across the glass counter. No, that wasn't likely. Surely if Jason was getting ready to propose, he'd have asked Ginger to design the ring. And yet, she hadn't mentioned a thing.

Footsteps approached, and I tried to hide the smile that was bursting through.

Wendy appeared before me. "What are you grinning at? Siccing Mrs. DeLeon on me?"

I laughed. "Oh, Wendy. Sorry. I couldn't resist, plus she was pestering me about when Jason is going to pop the question."

"It better be soon. He'd be an idiot to let you go." Wendy suddenly took a step back and evaluated me. "What style dress do you want?"

I inwardly cringed. Wendy's new hobby was sewing, and she fancied herself a dress designer, but the truth was she barely knew the difference between a straight stitch and a whip stitch.

She grabbed the fabric measuring tape that was constantly slung around her neck these days and moved toward my waist.

I stepped back. "Wait, wait. Let's not jinx anything. It just that he's been hinting around and he's making me dinner and tonight—"

Wendy squealed and wrapped her arms around my neck. "OMG! You'd better call me first thing."

The sound of high heels clicked on the tile floor. "Call you first about what?" Ginger asked.

"She'll call me first after the proposal," Wendy said.

Ginger and Wendy were on-and-off-again friends and sometimes got a little competitive when it came to attention from me. I suddenly found myself in a tug of war between the two.

"She'll call me first!" Ginger said. She quirked an eyebrow at me and said, "Right? I'm her best friend."

Wendy stepped in and put an arm around my shoulder. "Well, I'm her sister-in-law. Family trumps friends; everyone knows that."

Ginger grabbed my other arm. "No. Not true— "

I wrapped an arm around each of their shoulders. "Okay, as soon as he asks, I'll conference you both or"—I laughed—"send you a group text."

Dad popped his head into the back room. "For goodness sake! What are the lot of you doing back here? I have biddies bidding on baubles, ready to overpay and rip each other's gizzards out over these trinkets. Now get out there and close those sales!"

We laughed.

"Great pep talk, Dad," I said.

He ignored our laughter and began to usher us toward the sales floor. "Hurry now, Mrs. Harvey needs to be rung up for the nugget I just sold her."

Ginger looked offended. "But I thought she was interested in the emerald tennis bracelet I designed for her." She scurried off behind Dad.

Wendy and I followed, but she hung back a bit and said to me, "I got a text from Ben." She rolled her eyes. "You'll never believe it, but more changes for Living History Day."

Living History Day was an annual event where the entire town dressed up in 1850s garb that Wendy helped sew. It was a huge fair complete with sawmill demonstrations, tours of famous gold mines, historic reenactments, and gold panning. And, of course, lots of tourist memorabilia and junk food, topped off with a healthy dose of live music.

Our mutual friend, Ben, and his band *Oro Ignited* played every year.

"What's going on?" I asked.

Mrs. Jeffries, still clutching the diamond-encrusted gold nugget, spotted me and waved frantically at the glass counter. "Frannie! Show me those gold coin earrings! I think they'd make quite a match with this knickknack." She wiggled her wrist so the nugget moved back and forth hypnotist-style.

I moved across the sales floor and behind the counter as Wendy followed me.

"His band's been canceled," Wendy said.

I pulled the earrings for Mrs. Jeffries, who was now absorbed in our conversation.

Mrs. Jeffries pursed her lips. "More problems with Living History Day?"

"Problems with Dale Myers more specifically," Wendy answered.

Dale Myers was the new chairman for Living History Day.

"Dale Myers!" Mrs. Jeffries spat. "That man is making so many enemies. Why, I wouldn't be surprised if he winds up murdered! Did you know that my dear Mr. Jeffries and I were all set to sing for the event?"

"Were?" I repeated.

Mrs. Jeffries nodded, her expression changing to resemble that of a moping child. "Dale said that there were already too many acts scheduled and that he'd have to bump Edmond and me off the list.

Can you imagine? We've been singing on Living History Day for twenty-five years." She crossed her arms with a huff. "Not a very nice thing to do to us when we've just reached our quarter-of-a-century singing anniversary."

Wendy shook her head. "It's downright cruel if you ask me. Such a shame."

The Jeffries were by no means an act that would make it on Broadway. But they had a familiar, hometown sound and I couldn't imagine Living History Day without it.

"That's strange he would say that there are too many performers," I remarked. "I mean, if you two got bumped off the program and now Ben's band too, we won't have any entertainment."

Mrs. Jeffries looked down at the earrings Wendy had just handed her. "You're exactly right." She released a long-suffering sigh as she held the earrings up so that they sparkled in the sunlight streaming through the window. "I came in here to forget about all this. But Dale Meyers's doom and gloom managed to follow me here too."

Wendy offered a sympathetic smile. "I'm sorry about that. But don't you love those earrings? They're just the thing to cheer you up."

Mrs. Jeffries' face brightened considerably. "Yes.. . . . yes, I think you're right. I'll take them, Wendy!"

I barely hid my laughter at how quickly Mrs. Jeffries was consoled by the purchase. I supposed that it didn't matter what sold Ginger's jewelry so long as the afternoon was a success. Still, Dale Meyers had cast quite a shadow, and it seemed Ben wasn't the only one who was unhappy about it.

PREVIEW OF DYING FOR GOLD

CHAPTER 2

*A*t six p.m., we finally ushered everyone out of the store. Three cases of champagne later, we'd rung in one of our best nights for fine jewelry. Dad was grudgingly pleased, even if gold had taken a back seat to fine stones for one day.

Ginger was beside herself, squealing every three minutes. "We need to go out and celebrate!"

"I have a date with Jason," I said, pressing my hand against my tummy to quell the butterflies.

Tonight could be the big night!

"Right, right," Ginger said. She glanced over at Wendy. The two never went out without me, but it seemed that the day had been so successful that they might be gearing up for it. "Well, do you want to get a glass of Chardonnay with me over at the Wine Jug?"

Wendy shrugged. "Sure, why not? I've tolerated you all day. I might as well tolerate you a little longer." Ginger giggled as if Wendy had been joking.

I pinched Wendy. "Be nice."

Wendy laughed. "Okay, I'm just kidding. Besides we need to be together so you can call us when you get your big news."

I slipped my cell phone into my pocket.

"Don't worry, I'll call you guys. How late will you be at the Wine Jug?"

"Late," Ginger said. "We're celebrating. We're going to be late."

Wendy glanced at her watch. "Well, my darling husband will be home from the mine—"

Ginger grabbed Wendy's arm. "No you don't. If we go to the Wine Jug together, you can't ditch me."

"I'll walk with you guys since it's on my way to Jason's," I said, wiggling my fingers in Dad's direction.

Dad, who was closing down the final till, said, "See you in the morning. Don't stay out too late."

I hadn't exactly told him that I expected Jason to propose tonight. I knew Dad wasn't very fond of the idea of Jason and me getting married. Dad wanted me to marry again, sure, but Jason's career goals were not part of Dad's overall plan. Dad had made it clear that he wanted me to stay in Golden and run *The Nugget*, and Jason was in line for a promotion and the new position included moving to New York City.

As it happened, I personally loved the idea of moving to New York. The Big Apple was glamorous: skyscrapers, fine dining, Fifth Avenue department stores with designer names, theater, and opera.

All we had designer in Golden were secondhand goods sold in a small store around the corner from *The Nugget*. If you wanted to do any real shopping, you had to head down the Sierra foothills and into Sacramento to hit a mall. But even then, it wasn't nearly as sophisticated as New York.

Ginger, Wendy, and I walked the steep and windy streets of downtown Golden, passing the Chocolate Shoppe, the antique clocktower, and the theater. Dusk was falling, and one by one, the vintage lampposts that lined the narrow walkways flickered on.

We stopped in front of the Wine Jug before saying goodbye.

"Call me first thing," Ginger said, pushing open the door to the bar.

Wendy followed her in, but not before turning around and mouthing to me, "Call me first!"

I waved at them and then proceeded up the hill toward Jason's apartment. It was strange that he and I hadn't spoken all day, but maybe it was because he had a surprise in store for me . . .

Like a proposal.

I pushed the thought out of my mind. No need to go overboard with anticipation. If the time was right, Jason would know.

I'd been married before, but only for a short time. We'd both been straight out of high school and considered it a *starter* marriage. At least that's what everyone else called it, I think partly to make me feel better. Being a divorcée at twenty-one is not exactly what a girl dreams about, and it still broke my heart to think about how quickly it all fell apart for us. But things were different now.

This time around it'd be forever.

I turned the corner on Jason's street and climbed the rickety staircase to his apartment. In real estate lingo, they'd call the staircase *original*, but in reality it was one board shy of a full disaster.

I pressed the doorbell, waiting for Jason to answer. After a moment, the door flew open and my boyfriend appeared. There was stubble on his normally clean-shaven cheeks, his shirt was wrinkled, and he looked like he hadn't slept in twenty-four hours.

Ah! My computer genius.

I pressed my lips to his. "What's going on, Jason? You're a mess. Did I wake you?"

He dragged a hand across his blond hair. "No, um, I've been working. You know, I'm focusing on that promotion, so I was . . ." He shrugged his shoulders. "Did we have plans for tonight?"

"Yeah." My heart sank. He'd forgotten our date altogether. So much for a proposal. "I thought we were going to have dinner."

"Oh." He looked befuddled. "Um." He scratched his head. "I think I've got a box of pasta somewhere. You want to have spaghetti and sauce?"

"Hmm. Spaghetti and sauce sounds appetizing," I teased, poking him in the ribs, but he looked more offended than happy.

"Come on in," he said.

I followed him into his apartment. There were papers strewn across his coffee table, and his laptop was open and buzzing.

Jason did a little a jig and rotated his body so that it blocked my view of his screen. He seemed a little jittery.

Why was he acting so strange?

"Are you even hungry?" I asked.

"I could eat," he answered. "You know, I can always eat."

He padded over to the kitchen and waited for me to follow. He pulled open the refrigerator door. There was a half-full bottle of Chardonnay and a carton of eggs. Aside from that, the refrigerator was empty.

"I cleaned out the fridge earlier," he said.

"Do you want to go out to eat?"

"Out?" He suddenly looked ashen. "Uh, you know, I'm working on this project. I don't think I have time to go out. I'll miss my deadline."

"Well, I could fry a couple eggs for us," I said, ignoring the unsettled feeling creeping into my heart.

He rocked from his toes to his heels and then back again. "If you're hungry, that's fine. Or we could order takeout."

Jason was always ordering takeout, the ultimate bachelor. I figured one day when we were married, I'd show him what a regular Martha Stewart I was. I could cook with the best of them. I opened the small cupboard that made up his pantry.

"Let's see if I can find some beans and salsa or something. I'm sure I can make something yummy out of those eggs."

"No, don't bother. It's kind of a hassle to cook." He pulled out the bottle of Chardonnay and poured a glass for me.

"It's only a hassle to cook if you're not hungry," I said.

"I am hungry," he admitted.

"Well, then I'll make something." I rummaged a bit more through his cupboard and came up empty-handed. "If you had some chorizo and peppers, I could make you *Huevos a la Flamenca.*"

"I love it when you talk sexy to me," he said, pouring himself a glass of Chardonnay.

I socked him in the shoulder. "It's not sexy, it's Spanish."

"Same thing."

"I guess we'll have to settle for fried eggs. You do have oil, don't you?" I asked.

He pinched the bridge of his nose as if the mere thought of groceries or anything to do with cooking gave him a migraine. "I dunno."

"It's okay. I can poach the eggs." I grabbed a pot and filled it with water as I brought him up to speed on the success of the sale and the overall events of the day. I ended with telling him that Dale Meyers was making life a living hell for the Living History Day.

Jason sipped his wine, then groaned. "Dale's a nightmare. He's making my life miserable too."

"How's that?" I asked.

Jason looked like his thoughts were a million miles away, then he said suddenly, "I've been so busy I probably haven't even told you yet, but my department head got transferred and now I report directly to Dale. It's him who's going to decide if I get promoted or not."

"Oh, Dale's not so bad. I thought you guys got along. Wasn't he the one who hired you?"

Jason was a computer engineer who did his best work uninterrupted. It was sheer misery for him to go into an office and meet with the business team, but once he and Dale met, Dale had arranged for Jason to telecommute, and Jason hadn't stepped foot into the Sacramento branch in ages.

Jason paled. "Yeah. Seems like a long time ago, though. A lot's changed." He suddenly looked depressed.

"Why don't you go work on your project while I fix the eggs?" I suggested.

His eyes lit up. "Oh . . . you don't mind?"

"I'll call you when dinner is ready." I kissed his cheek.

He kissed me back, saying, "You're the best," then disappeared to the front room where his laptop beckoned.

I proceeded to fuss about the kitchen and wipe down the counters with a paper towel. When I went to toss the paper towel, I noticed his garbage was full.

If things went according to plan, soon this would be *our* garbage! Our *New York* garbage!

Oh, who cared if Jason was busy with work tonight. Soon we'd be married. Of that I was sure.

I tied the kitchen garbage bag up and headed down the back steps where the larger trash bins for his apartment were kept: a black one for refuse, a green one for compost, and a blue bin for recycling. All the bins were stationed along the alley next to his apartment building. There was a little trail of dark droplets along the alley that lined up right to the black garbage bin.

Yuk, someone must have had a leaky bag.

I popped open the lid of the trash can and spied a man's shoe.

The shoe might as well have been connected to an electrical current, because it gave me a shock of unmeasured proportions.

What I'd considered to be garbage refuse alongside the trash can I now realized were droplets of blood.

Oh no!

What was a bloody shoe doing in Jason's trash can?

I dropped the kitchen trash bag in the alley and studied the shoe a moment, a thousand thoughts zinging through my head. I grabbed a nearby stick and prodded at the shoe. When I moved it, blood oozed out.

A chill zipped down my spine.

Whose shoe was this?

How did it get here, and why?

Suddenly, a loud bang echoed down the street and the thought struck me that I might be in danger. I slammed down the lid and raced back up the stairs to Jason's apartment.

"Jason," I screamed as I pushed open his apartment door.

He appeared at me side immediately and grabbed my arms. "What's going on? What's wrong?"

I was shaking uncontrollably, adrenaline coursing through my veins. "I went to take down your garbage . . . I . . . there's a . . . and some blood . . . I . . ."

"What? Slow down, Frannie. Calm down." He hugged me to him, the warmth emanating from his body soothing me as I took a deep breath.

"I found a bloody shoe in your garbage can," I mumbled into his chest.

He pulled away from me and looked me in the face. "You found some blood in my garbage can? It's probably from the ground beef I tossed yesterday."

"A shoe. A bloody shoe."

I must not have been making any sense, because he blinked at me, then shook his head.

"Why don't you have a seat, Frannie? Did you fall on the stairs and lose your shoe?"

"No, not *my* shoe!" I sat on his couch and stuck out my Jimmy Choo clad feet. "Someone else's shoe. A man's shoe."

He shrugged. "I don't know. Maybe someone threw away an old shoe."

"It looked new."

He sighed. "Babe—"

"And there was blood on it!"

He waved a hand at me, dismissing my fear. "I told you I cleaned out the fridge earlier. I threw out some ground beef. Probably the blood from that dripped on it or something. Look, I have to get this project done. Why don't you just chill a bit? Have some more wine and relax."

"No! You have to go see. What if there's somebody skulking around downstairs!"

He made a face.

I felt like an idiot. He had work to do, and here I was probably overreacting. Suddenly, my fear was gone, but I still needed to be sure of what I'd seen.

He sat down on the couch and pulled me to him, embracing me. "Babe, you know this promotion is important, right? It's the way we get out of this town and to the Big Apple."

"I know."

He pressed his lips to mine. "You do still want to go with me, right?"

"Of course."

"Will you feel better if I go and check out the bloody shoe?"

I laughed. "You're making it sound like a stupid joke. Remember the one about the bloody finger?"

He frowned.

I rolled my eyes. "It's the one where the girl is alone and she gets the call." I made my voice low. "This is the bloody finger . . . and I'm one block away."

He shook his head. "It sounds like a pretty bad joke."

"It is," I agreed. "The girl gets the call three times and gets more scared each time, and then a guy with a small cut on his finger arrives on her doorstep and asks for a Band-Aid."

Jason buried his head in his hands. "Worst. Joke. Ever."

"I know. It's Ginger's favorite, and she's probably told it a million times since we were kids. Every Halloween especially."

Jason rose from the couch. "Okay, I'll check it out." He made his voice low and dramatic. "The bloody shoe."

He left the apartment, and I paced.

Why was there a bloody shoe in his garbage can? I walked to the front window of the apartment and looked out into the dark street. No one seemed to be around. Certainly no one stalking the building or anything else.

I grabbed my phone and sent a group message to Ginger and Wendy:

NO PROPOSAL YET BUT FOUND SOMETHING STRANGE IN THE TRASH.

Wendy texted back first.

A RECIEPT FROM A FINE JEWELER?

Ginger texted.

A USED NAPKIN FROM THE WINE JUG WITH SOME FLOOZY'S NUMBER?

Before I could reply, Jason came back into the room. "There's no shoe in the garbage, Frannie."

"What? It's gone?"

He shrugged. "I guess so. Now we have the case of the missing shoe."

How could it be gone?

"Are you sure you looked in the garbage can? The black one. It was inside, not on top."

"Yeah, I looked inside. You left my garbage bag in the alley, by the way, and Terrance's cat was already clawing it."

Terrance was Jason's downstairs neighbor.

"Anyway," Jason continued. "Since when do you take out my trash?"

I shrugged, poured the last few drops of Chardonnay into my glass, and shook the bottle, hoping for more. I didn't want to confess that I'd been fantasizing about domesticity, so instead I said, "I was bored."

He crossed his arms. "Sorry I can't entertain you, babe, but you know—"

"I know. The promotion."

He wrapped his arms around my waist and pulled me close to him. "One more week and everything will be different. I promise," he whispered into my ear.

I pressed my cheek against his, the stubble of his beard scratching my skin.

"Why don't you go meet up with Ginger and Wendy? I won't be offended," he said.

"No! I'm not going to leave you alone on a Saturday night!"

He laughed. "Babe. I got my work. I feel like I'm the one leaving you alone. I'll walk you to the Wine Jug."

"You don't have to walk me."

"Are you kidding? I gotta make sure you leave." He chuckled at his joke, but it left me feeling unsettled.

PREVIEW OF DYING FOR GOLD

CHAPTER 3

I screamed as someone grabbed me from behind.

The light in the Wine Jug was nonexistent. Okay, you could see, but barely. I always did better after my eyes had a chance to adjust, but Ginger and Wendy tackled me before that happened.

Ginger giggled. "What are you so skittish about?" she shouted over the band, *Oro Ignited*, which was playing on the small stage in the corner of the bar.

Wendy dragged me to their table and poured me a glass of a local white Zinfandel. The golden hills of California were fast becoming a mecca for small wineries that couldn't afford the high real estate prices in Napa and Sonoma counties. It seemed that every day a new tasting room was popping up, and we were the happy beneficiaries.

The wine was a bit too sweet for my taste, but it was cold, and I wasn't in a complaining mood.

"I found a bloody shoe in Jason's trash."

Ginger frowned. "Was it an old shoe or what? What do you mean bloody?"

"It was a man's shoe. New shoe. Expensive. It looked like there were drops of blood on it. I told Jason about it, and when he went to check it out, it was gone."

Wendy refilled her wine glass. "Who cares about an old shoe? What happened with Jason? Did he pop the question or what?"

I shook my head, suddenly feeling self-conscious.

Ginger reached for my hand. "It's going to happen, honey. Be patient."

I nodded, trying to hide the disappointment that was surging in my body. I swallowed hard, and before tears could come, I decided to change the subject back to safe territory. "The whole shoe thing is pretty weird, huh? I can't believe Jason didn't find it. I have to go look again myself," I said over the music. Suddenly, the band took a break and I found myself still yelling, "Will you come with me?"

My face flushed as all eyes turned toward me. I smiled at the neighboring tables and then sipped my Zinfandel.

The crowd got noisy again, and Wendy leaned in. "You mean go back to Jason's and poke around his trash? No way!"

Ginger flashed me look that I interpreted as she'd go with me later when we dropped off Wendy. I nodded at her, and she winked at me conspiratorially.

Wendy was too delicate to go digging in someone's trash. Even if that someone was my intended, or soon-to-be intended.

"Come on, you're good at digging," I teased her.

"Gold digging maybe." She smiled and batted her false eyelashes at me.

"Or digging for gossip," Ginger added. "She's great at that."

"A girl has got to have special talents in life," Wendy said.

I grabbed a couple of peanuts from the bowl in the center of the table and a strange sensation tingled through me.

What if Jason was in danger?

Ben, the lead singer of *Oro Ignited* and friend to everyone in town, sauntered over to us. "Evening, ladies. Evening, Frannie." He flashed me a strange, shy look that I couldn't interpret, then turned his attention to Ginger. "I heard your jewelry designs are the hottest fad in town." He took an empty chair from nearby, spun it around, and seated himself at our table with his arms and chest resting on the back of the chair.

Ginger grinned as wide as the Cheshire cat. "Who, pray tell, told you that?"

"My Aunt Jeannie was at the sale today. She brought a flashy pendant, and now my mother is scheming to steal it . . . I mean, borrow it from her."

While Ginger made small talk with Ben, Wendy leaned over to me. "So, what's up? Why do you think Jason didn't propose tonight?"

Her question poked at a sensitive part of my heart, and I suddenly felt hollowed out. I would have much preferred to dwell on the mystery of the bloody shoe than the mystery of the missed proposal.

I'd been so sure. All signs pointed to go, and yet . . .

I shrugged and felt my eyes start to fill.

Wendy grabbed my hand. "Oh, honey! Come on." She pulled me to my feet and led me to the ladies' room. Under the fluorescent lights, I looked like the wreck of the Hesperus.

"No wonder he didn't propose! Look at me!" I yelped.

Wendy laughed and smoothed down my hair. "You be quiet. You look fine."

While Ginger had always been my closest girlfriend and had nursed me through my shares of broken hearts, Wendy was a more recent addition in my life. Being that she was married to my brother and we worked together on a daily basis at The Nugget, I was finally starting to feel like I could confide in her.

I collapsed onto the chaise in the ladies' room and sighed. "I'm not giving up. I'm still sure he's the one, but he's under a lot of pressure is all. I think next week, after he gets the promotion . . ."

Wendy ran some tap water and wet a paper towel. She quirked a brow at me as she pressed the towel to the back of my neck. "You can have anyone in town, darling. I don't want you to settle."

I frowned. "I'm not settling! I love Jason."

She nodded. "Of course you do. What about Ben? Have you noticed the way he looks at you?"

I felt a surge of defensiveness. "I love Jason. He's the one."

She dabbed delicately at her lips. "Right. Ben and I were talking earlier. He and I made a deal."

"What about?" I studied Wendy's reflection in the mirror,

164

wondering what was coming next. Ben had been best friends with my first husband, but they'd parted ways more or less about the time of our divorce.

"He wants me to use my power of influence with Dale Myers to get his band back on the main stage for Living History Day."

I snorted. "What power of influence?"

Wendy laughed. "Well, I am in charge of all the costumes. Don't you think the threat of having everyone dance around naked is substantial?"

We giggled. The kind of infectious, delirious laughter bubbling through us after a stressful day was enough for us to slump together and wipe the tears dry.

Taking advantage of her good mood, I said, "Come with me to have a look in Jason's garbage can."

Wendy scrunched up her nose. "I told you. I'm not digging through someone's garbage."

"You don't have to dig through his garbage. I just want to see if the shoe is there." She looked unconvinced, but I laced an arm through hers and pulled her out of the ladies' room. "What are sisters-in-law for anyway?"

"Not this!" she protested, but she didn't untangle her arm from mine.

"I won't tell," I urged.

She snickered. "Your brother would die if he knew I was digging through someone's trash."

"I know, I know. You're a gold digger, not a trash digger," I teased.

She pinched my arm. "Shut it, sister."

I laughed, but she only pinched harder until I said, "Ouch! Okay, okay, I take it back, humorless."

Back at our table, the entire band had joined Ginger for cocktails. She was flirting outrageously with all of them, sitting on someone's lap while another guy rubbed her feet. I knew I'd never be able to convince her to leave with us. Instead, I wiggled my fingers at her in farewell. She made a phone receiver out of her hand and gestured that she'd call me later.

Wendy and I exited the Wine Jug, the cool night air a reprieve from the stifling atmosphere of the bar. We walked down the streets of Golden arm in arm, Wendy chatting about the costumes she was finalizing.

Even though I tried to focus on her chatter, my mind was on the bloody shoe. When we turned the corner to Jason's block, a chill crept up my spine. What exactly was I going to do with the shoe if I found it?

We entered the alley, and a cat hissed at us, then ran off.

A black cat no less.

Wendy screeched, "Bad luck!"

I poked her in the ribs. "Don't worry about that. It's the neighbor's cat." I said it to calm her down, but the truth was I was superstitious too.

The alley was curiously clean. There were no drops of blood like before. It was as if someone had scrubbed the concrete clean.

I flipped open the lid of the black garbage can.

There was no shoe. There wasn't anything, not even garbage.

"How weird! It was here," I said to Wendy.

"Where?" she asked.

"The place is spotless. Garbage pickup isn't until Monday," I said.

"Somebody must have picked it up," she answered.

I looked through the other bins quickly. The recycling and compost bins were half-full and seemed the same as before. "It doesn't make any sense. Does it?"

"No," she said. "It doesn't make sense that you would drag me out here to look at an empty trash can."

I poked her shoulder for her to be quiet, but she was just getting started.

"It's like the time you hauled me over to the Dress Stop to rummage through the sales bins when the sale was already over. Do you remember? Or the time—"

I pulled out my phone and quickly dialed Jason, glaring at Wendy and shushing her as I left a voicemail for Jason.

"He didn't answer," I said. "I'm going to go up and see if he's okay."

Wendy flashed me a look of concern. "Why wouldn't he be okay?"

"I don't know. I'm sure he's okay. That's not what I meant. I guess I'm just freaked out."

She shrugged. "I know you were hoping for a proposal, sweetheart, but sometimes the men, they keep us waiting. Give him some space. Do you know how long it took your brother to propose?"

I wasn't about to get into this conversation with Wendy again, so I said, "Speaking of which, George is probably back from the mine and wondering where you are."

"Right. I'd better go." Wendy wrapped her arms around me and gave me a squeeze. "Walk me to Pine?"

Pine Street was only a short way down the street, and from there we'd head in different directions. We walked in silence, then said goodbye at the intersection. I knew she'd asked me to walk her this way so that she could ensure I'd head home instead of going back to Jason's.

I watched her leave, and when she rounded the next corner, I doubled back toward Jason's apartment. It wasn't worth discussing with Wendy. She didn't understand that I needed to see him again.

I rounded the corner and sat on the steps of his apartment house and called his cell again.

No answer.

He was probably working, and it would be pushy of me to intrude. After all, I'd already called him twice. Still, the matter of the garbage being whisked away was bothering me. What if something had happened to him?

No, I was being ridiculous.

I fidgeted on the stairs, not knowing whether to go up or not. I imagined Jason surprising me at the top of the stairs with a ring. Although he had been rather standoffish tonight, could it be he had a black velvet box hidden somewhere in his apartment and was waiting for the right time to ask me?

He was probably waiting for his promotion. Maybe he'd surprise me with the news of the promotion and then pop the question. Yes, that's probably how it'd go down. Jason would make reservations at the local chophouse for Friday night. That seemed fancy enough. It wasn't New York City fine dining, but at least they had white tablecloths.

Then Living History Day on Saturday; it could be my going away party from Golden. All my friends would be there, and maybe *Oro Ignited* would play after all. I'd be able to say goodbye to everybody in style with a big fat diamond on my hand.

Oh, where was Jason?

I dialed his number again.

No answer.

Forget it. I climbed the steps to his apartment and knocked at the door. "Jason?"

Silence.

He's probably wrapped up in his work.

Still. I had to at least see him one final time before heading home.

My forgetful computer genius kept an extra key under his mat. It seemed that all he could keep track of were formulas and advanced algorithms. Forget about keys and wallets. I unearthed the key, stuck it in the door, and slowly pushed it open.

I peeked my head in. "Honey."

No answer.

I tiptoed into the apartment. It was eerily quiet.

"Jason?"

Still no response.

I walked to the living room; his laptop was still aglow.

Where was he?

He'd probably gone out to get something to eat. Maybe he was at *The Spoon*, our local burger joint, enjoying a greasy cheeseburger and all the fries he could stuff into his face.

I turned on my heel and headed toward his bedroom, still calling out to no avail, "Jason?"

Before I could push open the door to his bedroom, my phone buzzed. Jason's face illuminated the screen. "Hello?" I said into the phone.

"Frannie, where are you?" Jason asked.

"Where are *you*?" I asked.

"I'm at the Wine Jug looking for you."

"Oh! I came back to your place. I was worried about you," I said.

"My place?"

Was I imagining it, or was there a tone of panic in his voice?

"Yeah. I used your key from under the mat. I got worried about—"

"Worried? Uh . . . stay there! I'll be right back," he said.

"Okay."

"Sit on the couch in the living room. I'm coming right now," he said.

"Alright, honey, no problem." The cell phone reception started to get spotty, our connection sputtering and cracking. "I'll see you in a minute," I said, ready to hang up.

"Wait for me in the living room," he said again.

"Right," I agreed.

"My bedroom's a mess," he added by way of explanation.

"Don't worry about that," I said.

Why was he all nervous and panicked? Was he hiding something in there? A black velvet box, perhaps?

We hung up, and I couldn't resist. I pressed my palm against the door to his bedroom and pushed it open.

The room was not messy at all. In fact, it was the opposite of messy. It was nearly empty.

The bed was made and a few file boxes were sitting between the closet and his nightstand, as if he'd been packing.

That was strange.

My stomach flip-flopped, an odd feeling spreading from my torso into my throat. Certainly he was planning on proposing, he was just packing up getting ready for our move to New York. That had to be right. He was packed up to move with me . . . *with* me, not without me.

Right?

I carelessly opened one of his dressers. It was empty—no socks, underwear, or small velvet box.

No!

There had to be a mistake. Jason wasn't going to leave without proposing. He was *going* to propose; we were moving to New York *together*. I knew that.

I slid open the mirrored door of his closet. Two dark suits hung side by side like lost, forgotten soldiers. The rest of his closet was packed up.

I swallowed the dread bubbling up inside my throat.

He was going to leave!

He was leaving me in Golden. He was taking off to New York after the promotion on his own. He hadn't said anything to me about packing.

A mixture of sorrow and rage boiled inside me. I kicked the trunk by the end of bed.

Was the trunk empty too?

Without hesitation, I yanked open the lid. An unexpected sight burned my eyes, and a bloodcurdling scream escaped my throat, leaving me woozy and aghast. Inside the trunk was the shoeless body of Dale Meyer.

KEEP READING!

$\mathcal{T}$o continue...

Click here to get your copy now.

OTHER TITLES BY DIANA ORGAIN

Third Time's a Crime If only love were as simple as murder…

Yappy Hour Things take a *ruff* turn at the Wine & Bark when Maggie Patterson takes charge

Trigger Yappy Salmonella poisoning strikes at the Wine & Bark.

A Witch Called Wanda Can a witch solve a murder mystery?

I Wanda put a spell on you When Wanda is kidnapped, Maeve might need a little magic.

Brewing up Murder A witch, a murder, a dog...no, wait...a man..no...two men, three witches and a cat?

Murder as Sticky as Jam Mona and Vicki are ready for the grand opening of Jammin' Honey until…their store goes up in smoke…

Murder as Sweet as Honey Will the sweet taste of honey turn bitter with a killer town?

Murder as Savory as Biscuits Can some savory biscuits uncover the truth behind a murder?

GET SELECT DIANA ORGAIN TITLES FOR FREE

*B*uilding a relationship with my readers is one the things I enjoy best. I occasionally send out messages about new releases, special offers, discount codes and other bits of news relating to my various series.

And for a limited time, I'll send you copy of BUNDLE OF TROUBLE: Book 1 in the MATERNAL INSTINCTS MYSTERY SERIES.

Join now

ABOUT THE AUTHOR

*D*iana Orgain is the bestselling author of the *Maternal Instincts Mystery Series,* the *Love or Money Mystery Series,* and the *Roundup Crew Mysteries.* She is the co-author of NY Times Best-selling *Scrapbooking Mystery Series* with Laura Childs. For a complete listing of books, as well as excerpts and contests, and to connect with Diana:

Visit Diana's website at www.dianaorgain.com.

Join Diana reader club and newsletter and get Free books here

Made in the USA
Columbia, SC
19 November 2022

71746934R00112